Alpha Squad

Vecto: Voyage

REID HEMPER

Alpha Squad – Vecto: Voyage
Published by Vic's Lab, LLC

Copyright © 2016 Vic's Lab, LLC

All rights reserved. This book or any portion thereof
may not be reproduced or used in any manner whatsoever
without the express written permission of the publisher
except for the use of brief quotations in a book review.

This is a work of fiction. Names, characters, businesses, places,
events and incidents are either the products of the author's
imagination or used in a fictitious manner.

Cover art by Elvis Esparago (vzilefreak).
Cover design by Debbie Bishop.
Editors: Carol Thompson and Vic Adams.
Artwork Copyright © 2014 Vic's Lab, LLC

Printed in the United States of America

First Printing, 2017

ISBN-13: 978-1-942178-03-3

Vic's Lab, LLC
P.O. Box 10865
Danville, Va., 24543
www.VicsLab.com
A light novel and superhero book community.

DEDICATION

For God and all of my readers on Wattpad.

01

Is it time?

A pair of red eyes lit a dark storage room. The head of Azmeck's robot slowly turned—it looked to the left, to the right and then twisted its head around. As far as its eyes could see were more machines. *They were all the same—mass manufactured,* Vecto thought. *I'm getting the impression I don't fit in.*

He was inside a robot—inside what appeared to be a spaceship. He had spent three days in confinement, yet he was conscious the entire time. The anger he once had eventually faded in the past three days, and he had heard all of what Crysilis and Azmeck had to say. He knew why Streamline had to stop him.

The dimensional field Crysilis had used on him had given him time to reflect. But the time rift only affected his shields. When his orb's self-sustaining Force Field Shields died from the lack of carbon, the barrier died as well. And now he was free to roam—albeit in a lousy machine.

The robot's head twitched under the control of Vecto.

Its arm rose in the air as Vecto looked over the poor workmanship. Morphaal and Sable were still on the loose. He still had to find them; he still had to locate Zendora, but he certainly wouldn't fight in this body, he thought.

Vecto commanded the machine to walk. The old robot budged, swiveled its arms in the air and slapped a nearby robot, but it couldn't move its legs. It appeared they were manually disabled.

"Apologies," Vecto said to the robot he'd hit, noticing it was unmoving and staring straight ahead. It was almost familiar to him.

There is only one way to fix this problem, Vecto thought. He brought the robot's hand out, pointed its fingers at its chest, and thrust them into it. Metal grinded as wires spewed from the machine, sparking light throughout the dark room. Vecto yanked with both arms, pulling at the chest to free the orb inside. At last, he could breathe. He was free from the carbonless coating inside of the machine that kept his shield abstained.

Vecto hovered out of the robot and floated in the air. The orb sparked, and his Force Field Shields returned. A small, thin layer fluctuated over the orb, feeding off the air. It would take an hour to fully regain the shields that way. He needed a better carbon source and, fortunately for him, there was an abundant source of it all around him.

"Mind if I borrow a few of you guys?" Vecto asked the machines filling the vast storage room and then sucked the carbon from their metal bodies.

"Next," one of the many guards said as he scanned passengers on the Corona ship. Long lines formed in every row, waiting to be granted a Travel Access Card, or TAC. It was a larger than usual crowd today, one of the guards noticed, perhaps due to fear of the A.S., he thought.

Vecto's orb peeked around the corner. There was no way he could get by without being noticed. Even if he rolled across the floor, he'd be suspicious. *Well, here goes*, Vecto thought. It would have been nice if he could've just slipped from the storage bay into the ship, but the only door he'd found out of that place led to the dock. Vecto had no choice but to board with the other passengers. He formed his outer shield into the shape of a human. The shield contoured to a desirable size as a flush of colors rolled across his shield. It formed the design of a full-body powersuit, red in color with a stripe down each side. He had modeled it after one familiar to him—a techsuit hanging in his creator's lab.

Confident his disguise would work, Vecto walked away from the wall and casually passed behind the guards dealing with boarding passengers. So far, so good.

"Hey, you!" one of the Corona guards said in his direction.

Vecto stopped and calmly looked his way.

"Oh, sorry, I thought you were somebody I knew."

Vecto nodded and continued to walk, relieved it was just a close call.

"Wait a minute," the guard said again. "Did we give you a TAC?"

Vecto paused but didn't answer.

"Let me see your card, just in case."

Vecto was caught red-handed. "I didn't get one," he said, focusing the sound of his voice to only emit from his mouth instead of all around. "You see, I had to go to the restroom and—" Vecto fibbed.

"Oh, well, come on over then," the guard said and waved.

Vecto hesitated as he slowly walked over. He scanned

the vast loading bay and tried to pick out a guy from the crowd. Several lines away, a middle-aged man with a goatee caught Vecto's attention.

"I'm sorry, I forgot some important documents …" the man said. He was wearing a shirt with a palm tree illusion designed on it, signaling with his hand that he would come back later.

It was Vecto's only chance.

"Hey, we ain't got all day," the heavily armored guard said impatiently.

Vecto squeezed in the front of the line as angry passengers bit their lips.

"I need to see your face and take your fingerprints," the guard ordered.

Vecto complied. Like retreating insects, his helmet appeared as if it was decomposing, revealing the image of a face—the one of the palm tree guy.

The guard raised a pin to scan his pupil, so Vecto quickly adjusted his eyes to that of the man he saw. It checked out, so the guard asked for Vecto's hand. Fortunately, Vecto had a glimpse of that as well. The suit over his hand retreated and Vecto placed his thumb on a card, creating the exact grooves from the zoomed image he had of the palm tree man.

"Hey, what gives?" a heavy-set woman blurted, scratching her arm and neck. "We shouldn't have to let this guy jump us!"

"Now calm down," the masked guard said and looked at Vecto. "OK, Mr. … Robert Newman, now would you please stand still as I do an X-ray." He pulled out a device that fanned out to do the scan. Vecto froze as he stared at it. This was something Vecto couldn't mimic.

"Come on! We ain't got all day!" the woman yelled,

shoving Vecto. His body singed her hand and Vecto exaggerated a lean forward, knocking the scanner from the guard's grasp.

"Hey! Would you calm it down!" the guard snapped at the woman, assuming she had pushed him over.

"That guy just burnt my hand!" she shrieked.

"I'm sorry, I—" Vecto falsely apologized to both.

"Here, here, just move along," the guard said and handed him his TAC.

Vecto stuck the device to his suit as directed and smirked, walking off, amused the distraction actually worked, appreciative of the woman's indirect assistance. He glanced back to see the woman wobble to the guard, wheezing. He had to be careful though. With the fine details he had to do to disguise flesh and hair, it was using more carbons, and he could tell that it had irritated the woman's skin.

Vecto wandered throughout the mile-long ship. Knowing Dr. Azmeck, it would take days before he came back looking for him. First he'd want to set up his lab and then he'd have to get him during boarding, per regulation. Vecto had plenty of time, he thought as he headed for the shopping plaza.

The plaza was a massive four-tier structure with wide-open space at the core between each level to show off the stars seen through the transparent top hull. At the bottom center was a walkthrough field dome with a large fountain and trees as décor—a sort of park area. There were heavy crowds at each level—people of every size, race, and type, even genetically altered ones. However, there were no machines roaming the ship. The purpose of X-ray scans was to keep robots in storage facilities. Machines were banned from mingling with humans on the ship due to past mutiny and sabotage. It was the reason for Vecto to keep his identity a secret.

Yet, his identity was discovered by a seven-year-old.

A boy wearing a toy infrared visor jerked his head around as he saw nothing through the visor but could see Vecto's face and body when lifting it up.

"Hey Daddy, Daddy!" the kid yelled as he rushed to his father and tugged the back of his dress suit. "I found an android!"

"That's nonsense, son," the father said, messing up the kid's hair as he rubbed it. "You know they're banned from here."

"But, but!" the kid said and looked back for the android.

Vecto smirked at the kid.

"But Dad!" the kid yelled.

"All right, all right!" the father said and leaned to his level. "So where's he at?" he asked to appease him.

"Right there!" The kid pointed, but Vecto was gone.

"Oh, I see," the father said, standing back up. "Come along, now."

"But I really saw him!" the kid whined.

It was yet another close call for Vecto. He simply blended in with the crowd—sort of. He formed the image of a helmet over his head as he stepped on the wide, slanted escalator platform to take him to the top floor.

Unwillingly, Vecto could hear the myriad of conversations around him. Everywhere he walked, he heard the busy noise of people scatter through his mind. It was overwhelming until a ship announcement sounded overhead, allowing him to focus his attention.

"The Corona exploration ship will be departing from Acaterra's orbit in fifteen minutes," the female computer voice said over intercom. "Please refrain from leaving the ship. Any problems should be reported to Corona personnel. Please enjoy your ride."

Sarah? Vecto knew he recognized that voice. Was it really her?

It had been a long time since he'd heard her. She used to be the A.I. system for the A.S.'s ship, the SS Gyro, but she was transferred here after Gyro's ship was destroyed—as her massive navigation database was well sought-after. But why should he have to be reminded of Gyro's death again? He shook the thought away, trying not to obsess over it. *Perhaps A.I. Sarah has the coordinates to Zendora,* he thought.

Vecto was lifted to the top floor, and he walked around, staring at a number of eateries. They had no meaning to him. He strolled to a railing and gazed at the floors below. They were littered with a variety of meaningless shops.

He had to think of a plan to find Sarah and get off this ship. But his thoughts were once again interrupted, this time by someone yelling at the tier below.

"Help! Someone stole my TAC!" the man yelled, frantically patting himself down and scattering his eyes across the floor to make sure he didn't drop it.

Vecto casually looked around for the culprit. He kept the image of the victim in his head as he scanned data from everyone's TAC. Dozens of images from the devices were quickly rummaged through until he came to a guy wearing a black trench coat. The device he had matched the victim's identity.

"It's the guy in the trench coat!" Vecto yelled out to the guy who lost his TAC, trying to do some good for a change. However, Vecto neglected to control his voice. It inadvertently echoed in everyone's ears, and the thief donned a mask and took off running.

I need to be cautious, Vecto reflected, turning around. But another kid stood in his way. This time it was a little girl in a pink dress.

"Hey, aren't you going to catch him?!" the girl asked, looking up at his suit as if he was some sort of superhero.

Vecto, noticing her concerned eyes, was reminded of how he used to be that hero. Maybe he could help after all. One more contribution to society. "Why not?" he replied, realizing he could risk his identity.

Vecto looked over the balcony to see the thief running through crowds of people too scared or not worried at all to do anything about it. He stood up on the rail and jumped off, landing heavily on the third floor far below, making a dent in the surface. With a whoosh, he took off after the thief as the little girl stared in amazement.

Looking back, the thief saw Vecto chasing him as he rushed to the edge of the floor. It was a dead end—but not for long. He lifted a device and shot a cord to the bottom floor on the other side, then attached the other end of the cord to the railing. Mustering the courage, he jumped over the rail and rode down the wire with the hand-gripped device, glided over the Central Park dome and detached the wire on the other side. He fell from several yards and rolled as he hit the ground, automatically picking himself up as he kept running.

Not wanting to make a bigger scene, Vecto took the slope, rushing by people but watching his speed. He ran at a reasonable pace, trying to catch up, but it could easily cost him the chance to snag him.

The thief looked back, shoving through people, amused that he shook the guy off his trail. When he looked forward, a red blur of an arm swung at him, hitting him in the face. The thief was knocked to the ground, holding his broken nose.

"Hey! Wha-what do you think you're doing?!" the thief yelled at the guy as if he was the bad guy. "You just busted my nose, creepo!"

"I'm sorry, but you need to return that TAC to its rightful owner," the figure in a red powersuit said.

It wasn't Vecto, it was another guy. Vecto ran to the scene and noticed a person in a red and white technical-looking suit had stopped the thief. He had brown, spiky hair and hazel-green eyes. His TAC said he was seventeen. The shades of colors on his suit were divided in odd-shaped panels, reminding him of stained glass. He watched as the unknown hero reached down and pulled the mask from the thief's head.

"Hey, watch it, bub! You're revealing my identity!" the thief argued.

Vecto immediately knew who it was. "Not you again!" he blurted, realizing it was Chais, the thief he had ran into several days earlier. *Some things never change*, Vecto thought.

"Do I know you?" Chais asked, unaware it was Vecto.

Vecto retracted his fake helmet to show the identity of Robert Newman so as to assure Chais he didn't.

The other guy butted in. "Why'd you steal it?" he asked. "Don't you know that stealing someone's identity is wrong?"

Vecto kept quiet from that comment though it wasn't directed toward him.

"What? I needed ID is all," Chais said as he stood up and wiped blood from his nose on his sleeve.

The guy offered him a cleansing wipe with a disgusted twitch to his lips.

Chais looked at it, thinking how strange it was for him to offer assistance after busting his nose but took it anyway.

"So how'd you get on this ship if you didn't have one?" the guy pressed on.

"What? Some idiot robot gave me a pile of weapons. Fetched quite a bit of credits, I might add. So I decided to go on an adventure—explore the universe, you know?" Chais used the wipe and winced when he touched his nose.

Vecto remained silent.

"And you couldn't afford a ticket?" the stranger asked.

"Wouldn't matter," Chais shrugged. "I'm not ID'd in the database. So I make a living on the streets."

The questioner shook his head and crossed his arms. "And what robot could have been ordered to sell you weapons?" he asked.

"I dunno. Some robo named Vecto," Chais muttered.

"Vecto?!" the guy blurted in shock as Vecto looked away, preparing for the worst.

"Yeah, he was cool and all until I found out he killed the SS6."

"He did what? No, he wouldn't do that. He's a member of the Alpha Squad."

"Well, sorry, pal," Chais said, dusting himself off. "Hate to bombard your dreams." He casually began walking off, tucking the bloody wipe in his pocket.

"Whoa! Not so fast!" the guy demanded and yanked him back. "You still need to return that TAC."

Vecto spoke up. "How do you know about Vecto?" he asked the stranger in the red and white powersuit, curious about his response.

"Don't you?" The guy shook his head. "Well, you know, the A.S. were the saviors of the omniverse at one time. I used to collect robotic figurines of Vecto when I was a kid. But that was over ten years ago, you know?"

"Wow!" Chaise said with a hint of sarcasm. "He was that big, huh? Too bad for him."

Vecto pressed on. "What else do you know about him?" It wasn't too often that he could get an outside opinion.

"Well, um, he wasn't like other robots," the man explained, scratching the back of his head. "He knew right from wrong, had emotions, and was kind of a hero to me." He lowered his head, wondering why he was having this unimportant conversation, but he at least wanted to share his little know connection. "But you know what? My dad used to know Vic—his creator, that is. And we even share the same last name—Vecto and I."

Vecto was in shock, if that was even possible. "So what's your name?" he asked, anticipating his response.

The guy ruffled his fingers through his brown spiky hair and reached his hand out. "I'm Erich Botland. Nice to meet ya!"

Yes, it was Erich Botland, the son of Durrick Botland, the man who befriended Vic—the man whose surname Vic named Vecto after!

Vecto didn't shake his hand, so Erich retracted it. "Yeah, my dad went to school with Vic," Erich continued his story. "He said that everybody picked on him 'cause he was this short Dinishman, but not my dad. I guess using our last name was a way to thank my father." Erich ruffled through his hair again. "Ah, why am I even telling you all this?" He reached his hand out again to shake. "What's your name?"

Vecto at last shook his hand briefly before responding. "Robert Newman."

"Robert, huh?" Erich mused over the name. "How about I call you Bob—no, how about Rob? Bob's too common."

Vecto nodded.

"Crap! Where'd he go?" Erich said as he looked around to find the thief.

"Not to worry," Vecto said looking behind him to see security guards approach Chais and slam him face first into a wall.

"Hey! You got the wrong guy!" Chais pleaded.

"Save it for jail!" one of the guards said as he put Chais' hands behind his back and stuck a disk on each of his wrists. The devices embedded in his arm and magnetized together. Vecto watched the guards pat him down and pull out device after device from his trench coat. But what struck his attention the most was the glare of diamonds.

It was in the shape of a cross.

A very familiar cross.

In no time, Vecto had Chais by the throat, slamming him against the wall. "Where'd you get that?" Vecto demanded.

"Break it up, gentlemen!" a guard yelled, reaching for Vecto.

Vecto let go before the guard touched him, grasping the cross and taking it away from Chais' pocket. He couldn't give away his identity, Vecto stressed to himself, keeping himself under control.

"What? Found it lodged in the ground at some destroyed base, is all," Chais explained nonchalantly as he took breathes of air, ignoring the sting of his throat.

Seeing that Chais' trench coat was loaded with gadgets, the guards removed the whole thing, unsnapping the magnetic cuffs for a brief second. It left Chais with a muscle-fitting, black, long-sleeved shirt, matching the color of his slightly baggy pants.

"I bet you looted the place, too, didn't you?!" Vecto yelled.

One of the guards grabbed the cross in Vecto's grasp. "I'm sorry, we'll have to confiscate this," he said to Vecto. The guard jolted as something heated through his armor.

"But that's—" Vecto stopped himself short, almost saying it was Gyro's. He couldn't say it without causing an investigation. He reluctantly complied, handing the cross over to him as the guard shook his hand in the air.

The Corona guard dismissed the incident as a malfunction in his suit's thermal setting and helped the others gather Chais' items into a retractable poll box. When done, the guards shoved the thief in front of them and headed off. Vecto could do nothing as he watched them take Chais away, along with the last remembrance he had of Gyro. It was if he was being punished for his crimes, unable to act on his free will due to his disguise. But it was more than that. It was choice he had to make, as all choices have consequences.

"Don't worry about it," Erich said, patting Vecto on the shoulder, reassuring him it wasn't the end of the omniverse. "Wanna grab a bite to eat?"

Moments later, Vecto sat at a table on the third floor. Not only was it awkward for him to remain in disguise, it was uncomfortable. Vecto had to put the thought of Gyro's cross aside and reminded himself to retrieve it at a later date. But he couldn't help but think of his so-far adventure—bypassing guards, hearing A.I. Sarah's voice after so many years, chasing after a thief who so happened to be Chais and, most intriguingly, meeting the son of the scientist he was named after. He almost felt as if he was living a new life—no one knowing who he was or what he did.

"Attention passengers," Sarah's voice said over the intercom. "This ship will soon be initiating a gravitation flux and will be traveling at velos speed. Please do not be alarmed, as there will be a slight jolt."

Vecto waited as the shift in force passed. It meant he would be stuck on this ship for a while. He looked over the table to see Erich coming back to introduce some friends of his.

"Hey, Rob!" Erich called out. "Let me introduce you to a couple friends I made on the ship."

"Ahoy, matey!" The older fellow walked over to Vecto and reached out his hand to shake. In fact, it was his only arm, Vecto noticed. The middle-aged man had an eye patch and long brown, braided hair, matching his lengthy beard. He wore old clothing with holes in them and had pierced ears—also with large holes. The only things he was missing was a hook.

"Hello," Vecto simply said and briefly shook his hand.

"Arrr! A mighty grip ye have, lad!" the man said, flinging his hand in the air. "Name's Captain Cutlass!"

Vecto didn't comment.

"And this is me hearty Trip, a true buccaneer!" the wannabe pirate said, motioning to his friend who paced their way.

Trip stared pointedly at the ground as he slowly walked, counting each of his steps. He wore neatly shined attire and had perfectly parted hair and yellow eyes. He came to the table and used a sanitary wipe chair.

"Arr, Trip! Why don't ye say 'ahoy' to the fella!" Cutlass said.

"Hel-hel-hello," Trip stuttered.

Cutlass cleared his throat and whispered to Vecto, "Don't mind he, my lad. Trip's a wee slow in the noggin."

Vecto disagreed. "He appears to have an obsessive compulsive disorder."

"Ehh? Now hold on thar."

Vecto was too monotone. What if Cutlass suspected he was a robot?

"Don't tell me yar a rich kid?" Cutlass asked. "'Cause I ain't got taste for those scallywag know-it-alls."

Vecto was safe. "Naa, naa!" he assured. "My aunt had autism and OCD like that. Just heard it from 'em." Of course, he didn't have an aunt, but Cutlass bought it.

"Arr, well tell ye aunt I said 'ahoy' when you see her, mate."

"She's dead," Vecto continued the lie.

"My! Sorry, me lad," Cutlass said, startled, sitting down.

That shut him up at least.

Erich took the last seat beside Vecto.

"So," Vecto said loud enough to gather their attention, "does anyone have any real names—besides Erich that is?" Vecto asked ironically considering his odd name.

Trip weakly rose his hand. "I-I do. Trip's my name. Trip Alloway."

"OK ..." Vecto took note and looked at Cutlass.

"Arr, well, see ... don't remember if I had one!" Cutlass said.

"You're name's Greg Jensen," Erich said for him as he laughed and gave him a friendly slap on the back. "Remember? Look at your TAC."

"Well blow me down!" Cutlass said as he checked his ID.

Vecto nodded. "It's nice to meet you all," he replied,

amused at the unique qualities of who appeared to be his new companions. "My name is Robert Newman."

"Much obliged, now let's bring on the rum and turkey!" Cutlass bellowed. "Me belly's a starvin'!"

Both Trip and Erich shook their heads as if to say, "Not again!"

Minutes later, three plates popped up from the center of the table—food for all but Vecto.

"If you're worried about credits, I can help," Erich offered when he noticed Vecto didn't order any food.

"I am fine," Vecto said. "I am not hungry."

Cutlass chewed his turkey with his mouth wide open and drank a glass of water. "Arr, stop ye kiddin'!" he said, "Take a bite!" He offered some of his bitten food.

"No thank you," Vecto replied.

"Now hold on thar," Cutlass said. "Yar not some scurvy-dog veggie lad, are ye?"

"You mean vegetarian?" Vecto couldn't help but correct him. "No."

"Then come on, lad! Eat up!" Cutlass demanded and threw his turkey on Vecto's plate.

Who had he heard that from? From Leroy Johnson, that's who. Out of respect, Vecto picked up the turkey. Instead of sucking the carbon from it, Vecto formed an esophagus with his shield and put the turkey in his mouth. But he forgot to chew and watched as the others stared at him in surprised silence for a second. Then Cutlass laughed heartily.

"Now that's the spirit!" Cutlass yelled as Trip looked disgusted.

"I-I can't believe you just ate after that-that … ribald slo-slo-slob," Trip said, looking away and sanitizing his hands.

Vecto thought that he should have at least tried to

chew, but it didn't seem as if they paid attention to that part. "Excuse me," he politely said and abruptly stood and left.

"He didn't mean it," Erich assured, wondering where he was going.

"Arr, it probably didn't settle well, and he went to the head," Cutlass said, meaning the "toilet," and took another gulp from his glass.

Sure enough, Vecto went to the restroom to dislodge the food from the pocket of his shield. He couldn't afford making any more mistakes. It was pertinent that he kept his identity secret. As fascinating as it was to meet Erich, he realized he must avoid human contact in order to remain anonymous. It was time for him to communicate with A.I. Sarah and find the coordinates of Zendora.

But like every other time he was about to do something, more danger arrived. The ship shook ... more violently than a simple exit from a graviton flux. Vecto looked around the stall, comprising of a frictionless funnel toilet and a force-field-enclosed stall. He knew the ship wasn't leaving the gravity well so soon. And it was unusual for a ship this large and advanced to jolt so heavily.

It was followed by Sarah's voice. "This is an emergency," she said. "Please return to your lodgings in a safe and orderly fashion. We assure you that we have the situation under control. Please return to your lodgings for safety. I repeat, this is an emergency."

A male's voice cursed in the stall next to Vecto. "Geez, can't a man go to the bathroom in peace?" The man walked out of the restroom, neglecting to sanitize his hands.

Vecto was calm as he did a MZI scan to form a Lapton map of most of the ship. It didn't take too long to see what the emergency was. The hull was breached, and enemy combatants were rushing inside.

Perhaps a little enemy hunting exercise would do him some good. He couldn't help but think they came searching for him. If only they knew who they were dealing with.

02

As Vecto left to fight the pirates, Erich, Trip, and Cutlass sat in a now-hectic plaza as the ship's A.I. voice once again boomed over the intercom.

"I repeat, please return to the residential section of this ship. This is an emergency, but we have the situation under control," Sarah's voice reiterated over the intercom.

The ship viciously quivered again.

"Thar she blows!" Captain Cutlass blurted out. He wobbled to stand up and stumbled into Trip. "Arr, all hands on deck!" Cutlass yelled, lifting his "rum" in the air. "Drop the sails and anchor. Man the guns and ready ye-self for battle!"

"Wou-would you qu-quit the antics!" Trip said.

Cutlass was right. They couldn't just stand around and get killed. But they had no idea what happened. And by the sound of it, it was likely a collision rather than gunfire.

"So wha-wha-what are w-we going t-to do?" Trip stuttered to Erich, shifting his eyes around as multitudes of people rushed by in panic.

Erich observed the myriad of occupants dashing for the escalator and hiding behind tables. "You heard the lady," Erich said. "The civilians need to evac to their shelters. You two can leave as well, but I'm going to help them."

"I-I-I'm not leaving wi-with-without you!" Trip asserted.

Erich looked across his shoulder at Trip. "Then you two can come," he said as he rushed toward the elevator to direct traffic.

"Yo-ho-ho, and a bottle of rum!" Cutlass cheered as Trip followed and Cutlass stumbled behind.

Erich, Trip, and Cutlass soon directed traffic into the heavily packed strip elevators, with all ramps switched to a downward motion. They helped the scared and confused calm down and lessened their panic. They were now on the second floor, guiding the citizens until several guards in hovering platforms finally rose to their level to help out.

"We appreciate the assistance," one of the Coronan guards said as he leapt off the platform. "Now please move along. We're taking over now."

"But wha-what happened to the sh-sh-ship?" Trip asked the guard.

"Nothin' to worry 'bout, kid," another said.

"If the ship has been breached, I can help," Erich offered.

The first guard looked over him and scanned his TAC. His face turned sour. "We have the situation under control, Mr. Botland. It's our duty to ensure the safety of all occupants, including you."

"But I can't just sit around and do nothing!" Erich argued.

He stopped as a woman rushed by in panic searching

for someone.

"My baby! My poor baby!" she cried out, looking for her son.

Erich glared at the guard and ran to assist. "Ma'am, calm down. What's the matter?"

"My baby boy, Timmy!" the woman cried out. "I can't find him!"

"Where was he at the last time you saw him?"

"I-I don't know!" she said starting to cry in distress. "On the floor above is the last I saw him!"

"Just stay with the guards," Erich said, "I'll find him."

Cutlass and Trip ran over to help.

"Arr, need any assistance, me lad?" Cutlass asked.

"You two can go on ahead," Erich said as he clicked a portion of his suit to activate his boosters. Two lengthy panels fanned up from the back of his Echelon suit as rockets ignited. Energy blasted to the surface and propelled him to the floor above, leaving his two friends behind. He hovered over the surface and cut off the boosters, landing on the third floor, which appeared littered with shopping disks and left-behind merchandise. The floor was empty, unlike the usual bustling crowd—as it had been completely evacuated and blocked off.

"Timmy?" Erich called out, slowly walking on the desolate floor. "Timmy, your mom has been worried sick trying to find you. ... I'm here to help you."

Nothing.

"Timmy, if you're hiding, don't be scared. I'm here to help."

Another voice echoed back. "If you're looking for the kid, I returned him to his father."

Erich looked down the wide hall, over toward the right half, to see a figure approaching. He wore a buttoned-up, white, tunic-like shirt and had a long black ponytail. He appeared somewhat Asian-looking, Erich thought, and was about his age, seventeen.

"Well glad you could help out," Erich said loud enough for him to hear as the guy approached. "The name's Erich Botland."

The man stopped and bowed. "You may call me Feit," he said. He then walked over to a railing and looked at the floor below. "Looks like they've about locked off the second floor now. Only one more to go."

"So do you know anything about the enemy?" Erich asked.

"Yes. They are pirates called the Blood Claw. They boarded the ship on portside, and it seems they plan to take it over."

"You mean they're on the ship?!" Erich said. He spun around to leave. "I gotta help fight them!"

"Don't worry," Feit assured him. "They're being—how should I put it—well taken care of. ... What we need to do now is—"

Before he could finish, the ship shook; this time the impact was closer, followed by another rumble. It was the sound of several blasts, striking the dome overhead. Erich and Feit quickly looked up to see a space shuttle headed for the dome in a head-on collision. The Corona wasted no time and fired back with streams of blue, red, and yellow energy, but it didn't stop the shuttle from coming. It was approaching fast, rapidly firing at the dome to break through, until at last it burst through the thick ceiling—not by the blast but by the sharp nose of the ship. It shattered yards of the thick, translucent, metal-like protective dome overhead—the only thing protecting the citizens below.

"Watch out!" Feit yelled. He grabbed Erich, using his

momentum to slide them to the center railing of the plaza. Their bodies slammed against the rail as the pirate ship smashed into the top floor. It crashed through the upper floor, sending metal shrapnel soaring as the roof above Erich and Feit subsequently collapsed. The seventy-foot long shuttle plunged in front of the two, grinding across the dented floor to a halt as broken pieces of the ceiling scattered. Smoke fumed from the ship, being sucked in with the air through the massive hole above.

Erich and Feit held tight to the rail as their bodies lifted from the suction. They could hear screams from far below echo closer as the tornado-like funnel snatched civilians. Erich couldn't bear to let them die. He clutched the railing and attached a wire from his wrist to it, then let go, flipped upside down, and activated his thrusters to go against the current. A panel popped up from the top of his wrist, and he fired pulse-wires, sans deadly energy. Four shot out; the tips from these tetralirium cords fanned out in midair and struck their bodies, molecularly binding to them. It didn't matter to Erich whether they latched to arms, legs, or backs—at least they hit their targets.

Many of the civilians were safe in the force-field-protected Central Dome Park at the center of the plaza, where they were to depart to their quarters. But others were not, and more were caught in the vacuum. Erich fired four more pulse-wires from his other wrist, each successful in grabbing people. But the momentum of their bodies was more than he could take. The wire connecting him to the railing snapped straight, yanking his arm.

Erich screamed in pain. He couldn't save them all. Several women, men, and children were helplessly sucked into space. Erich closed his eyes, unwilling to watch.

At last, the ship's safety shield activated. A force field

blocked the passage, followed by the loud hum of a massive barrier curving across the entire dome. It slid to the other side and snapped in place, sealing the gap and creating a blue emergency-light tint to the room.

The ship's gravity instantly took its toll, and Erich and the others fell. The pulse-wires snapped as he hung from the wire, followed by the weight of the citizens yanking his arms. Erich felt pain surge through both arms and his chest—like his arms were being ripped from both ends. They violently spun while they yelled. But that was the least of Erich's worries.

Erich bit his lip at the thought of the citizens he couldn't save, helpless as they were sucked into space without a thing he could do to stop it.

"Oh, thank you! Thank you!" an older woman yelled from below after her cries silenced. The others followed suit, thanking Erich for saving them—glad to be alive.

"Seems you saved the day, sir," a voice said.

Erich looked down to see Feit standing on the floor below, looking up at him with his hand reached out. "Need a hand?" he asked in a serious, yet teasingly, tone. "Come on and hurry down. Some of the pirate crew may still be alive."

Hearing of the pirates wasn't particularly exciting news, though.

"Just get us down from here!" an overweight person yelled.

"All right, all right," Erich replied. He unlocked the wires from his wrist and extended the wires to lower them. Feit helped them straighten up, and when they were safe, Erich detached the wires. He flipped backward and landed hard in a crouched position.

His wrists were throbbing.

"You did well," Feit said. "Quite impressive, I'd say."

"Yes! Land!" one of the civilians yelled and kissed the floor.

Erich slowly rose, shaking his head. "Yeah, but I couldn't save them all," he muttered quietly.

"Sometimes you can't," Feit said, nodding to several people as they thanked them and rushed off. "No one is all-powerful, and life is never predictable."

"Yeah, I guess," Erich said, flexing his fingers and moving his wrists to loosen the tightening pain. "And thanks for, um, helping out. I'm sure they appreciated it."

"You're the hero. I did nothing," Feit replied, straightening his tunic.

"Yeah, well, so anyways, what's up with that ship?" Erich asked and pointed at the wreckage nearby. It towered almost as high as the roof from the fourth floor.

Smoke fumed from the red and black exterior, but it was still intact. It meant they should have survived if the ship had internal impact absorption, yet not a single soul emerged from the enemy shuttle. Not yet, of course.

Erich pushed pressure spots on his Echelon suit to activate its battle functions. The suit's panels slightly buffed out as energy streamed between the cracks. A bright red spinning disk on his back powered it. Erich detached the pulse-wire trajectory panel going up his right forearm, revealing multitudes of exposed wires and mechanics. He took a cylindrical disk out and replaced it with another one from his belt. It snapped into place, and Erich reattached the panel to his arm.

Feit looked on with his arms behind his back, his ponytail slightly swinging behind. "Different wires?"

Erich lowered his arms. "You'll see." One wire crept from his right wrist, dangling to the surface. It glowed yellow. "You got any weapons?" Erich asked. "Or armor? I have a feeling the pirates aren't dead."

Feit shook his head. "I only need skill and a good environment."

"OK …" Erich said. A mask formed over his head. "Got a game plan, then?"

"I make it as I go," Feit responded, slowly walking to the red and black drill-looking ship. He stood in front of it and yelled at it in a composed manner. "Would you please come out, sirs? I don't have all day!"

A few more tense seconds passed, culminating with an explosion from the door. In in-sync fashion, suited pirates stormed from the downed ship, fanning out and discharging their automatic weapons.

Feit was now in the air, coming down on one of the pirates with his fist. He smashed his head in and spun the guy's body around to serve as a shield. Feit grabbed his gun, but didn't fire it. Instead, he slung it at a pirate's throat. Feit spun low and grabbed the body's leg. He spun around and slid the body across the floor to knock the pirates' feet from below them.

Close by, other pirates fired at Erich. But Erich was a step ahead of them. He spun the wire in the air like a propeller, letting yellow pulse energy trail behind and block bullets. When the bullet-storm stopped, Erich pitched his arm around and threw the wire at one of them, its yellow glow now gone.

It struck the pirate in the chest, knocking him into the hull of the pirate ship. The pirate looked down but was snapped forward by the string. Erich tossed him into the other pirates and detached the string, letting it wrap around his spinning body. The other pirates scrambled to their feet, and Erich launched several wires at them. The strings grabbed them by the chest—one by the face. Erich jerked the lines toward him and kicked the pirates as they approached. He detached the wires to let their bodies spin and wrap within the cords.

"Who's next?" Erich said as he glanced at the other pirates.

They opened fire.

With his mask on tight, he jetted for them as bullets and pulse-beams struck his plated armor. But he kept coming, enduring the hits, and drove a device into a pirate's chest. A virus overtook the pirate's suit and froze his body in place. Erich rushed at another man and slammed his fist through the guy's visor, releasing knockout gas for him to choke on. But another pirate fired from behind. Erich spun around and shot a wire at the gun, then tossed it from his hands as bullets scattered through the room. One of them struck Erich between two panels on his arm.

Erich felt the impact with a grunt and fell to his knees.

Coming from behind, a man kicked him in the back, striking his circular power source. Erich crashed to the floor. A hand grabbed him from the back of the head and slammed his face into the surface. Erich could hardly adjust as the mysterious pirate yanked him by the ankle and dragged him away.

Erich regained his thoughts and pushed himself from the deck to kick his attacker with his other foot. But the man swiftly let go of the ankle and grabbed the other one, then threw him into a nearby shop display window.

Erich rocketed through the display glass, clothes, and mannequins until he slammed into the back wall. His head pounded from the impact and his ears rang, but Erich shook off the pain. His Echelon suit had absorbed most of the impact, but his spine still stung as he attempted to sit up.

"Geez, who is this guy?!" he said to himself, grunting as he flung lingerie from his eyes. He gazed up to see the pirate. "It can't be."

The pirate tranquilly leaned on a manikin, waiting for Erich to stand. He had long, red hair flowing behind his helmet as an officer's symbol adorned his red suit. Slowly, he removed his helmet to reveal a pretty-boy face, ruined by the crazy smirk he had as he licked his pale lips.

Aaron? Erich thought, thinking he was a bounty hunter he knew. No, it wasn't him. This man was different. A modified clone, perhaps.

"I've seen your skills. You are a fool not to kill them," Mirth said. He burst into laughter and brushed his hair back as he sliced the manikin's head off with a quick swipe from his fencing-like sword. "When I kill you, the Blood Claw will still be alive to torture more innocent lives."

Erich stood to face him. "You guys are all the same. I just don't want to be like you."

"Then you're a fool!" Mirth blurted. He quickly slashed at Erich, but Erich jumped back to avoid the blade. Mirth came at him with one hand behind his back as if it was a fencing match. But Erich used magnetism from his palm to repel the blade away from him with each swing. Unable to strike, the pirate went for a thrust. Erich dodged it and kicked the sword from his hand. The tip pierced into a manikin's stomach, wobbling from the impact.

"Heh, heh. Impressive …" the pirate acknowledged. "You will be well fit to join the Blood Claw. We need new blood, per say." In a blur, Mirth grabbed Erich by the throat and yanked him off the ground, then spun around and threw him back out of the store. Erich's body smashed through more glass as Mirth walked to the manikin. He calmly placed his foot on it, yanked the blade out, and kicked the manikin aside. He walked overtop lingerie as he left through the store after Erich.

Erich's body tumbled across the third floor and barrel-rolled into Feit. Feit quickly regained his footing.

"Are you all right?" Feit asked, taking a quick glance.

"Yeah, sure," Erich said and forced himself to stand while holding his arm. "Not sure I have much energy left, though."

"You'll find some," Feit said, keeping his stance but glancing to his side to see the pirate, Mirth, approaching with his sword ready.

"My name is Mirth," the pirate said as he brushed his hair from his face.

"You look like you came from the spittin' image of a meric," Erich said, referring to ugly tentacle creatures.

"Touché," Mirth said. He checked his chrodometer on his wrist to tell the time. "However, I have stalled you long enough."

"What are you talking about?" Erich asked. His chest tightened in panic.

You didn't think we'd attack full force without a backup plan, now did you?" Mirth burst into laughter. "There were other pirates who exited our ship from the back, in civilian clothes, now mingled in the crowd, unnoticed!"

"What?!" Erich and Feit yelled together.

"For your information, our colleagues surrounded the guards. And on my signal, they'll open fire, eliminating resistance and killing the civilians below."

Erich tapped a panel on his side.

"So, as you see," Mire continued his monologue,

walking to a railing and looking below, letting strands of his hair flow in his face. "I have the power of their fate."

"Why are you telling us this?" Erich asked.

Mirth laughed as he calmly walked toward them. "So you will suffer as well, helpless to stop them!" Mirth pulled out a gun and fired near Erich's feet.

At the same time, Erich shot him in the forehead.

Mirth leaned forward and slammed into the ground headfirst.

Feit looked at Erich, surprised that he shot a man while Mirth hadn't aimed to kill.

Erich fell to his knees. He fell flat as something pulled him closer.

"The gravity …" Erich gasped.

Gravity? Feit thought. A gravity gun? He reached in his tunic and tossed a button at Erich to find out. The button quickly descended and slammed into the floor.

Feit walked over to the gun in Mirth's hand and studied the weapon. He turned a dial and Erich gasped in pain. He then pushed it inward and Erich breathed a sigh of relief.

"Ugh. Took you long enough," Erich said, slowly getting to his knees.

"So this is some sort of gravity gun," Feit said. "Interesting." He shot at Mirth's body.

"Hey, you're going to kill him!"

"Didn't you already?"

"No, I used a tranquilizer."

"You're too kind, Erich," Feit said. "If you let him survive, he will find a way to come after you—and kill more innocent lives while he's at it."

"That's not justice," Erich said as he stood.

"There is no justice," Feit said, turning the dial up. "It's called life.

"Please."

Feit pressed the button to deactivate the gravity pull. "Very well, sir. He won't haunt *me*."

"Thank you. Now about the others—" Erich said.

He was stopped short as he heard an explosion. Erich stumbled but gained his balance. He rushed to the edge to look down, only to see gunfire and screaming citizens on the bottom floor.

"That must have been the signal," Feit said. "Let's go, Mr. Hero!" He rushed for the escalator and slid down its rail.

"Right in front of you!" Erich said and tapped a panel on his shoulder to activate his rocket boosters.

Meanwhile, down below, the remaining civilians ran for cover as the guards and pirates battled each other with gunfire.

Cutlass and Trip were among the ones caught in the line of fire.

"G-g-get behind me!" Trip yelled. He snatched a small rod from his pocket and formed a body shield with it.

"Arr, now that's the spirit!" Cutlass cheered as he ducked flying bullets and hid behind Trip. "These yellow-bellied pirates be shark bait!" he yelled, then bit off a grenade pin and threw the explosive at the pirates. It went off and several bodies went sailing over their comrades' heads.

"Lo-lo-look who-who's talking," Trip cut back, maintaining the shield as some pirates died but the others retaliated.

"No, me hearty, these be Blood Claw pirates," Cutlass said. "They pillage ships."

"No-no-now's not the time!" Trip yelled back.

"But where be Rob?" Cutlass asked, taking off his old, torn shoe to grab a small tube from it.

"Wou-would you ju-just throw it already!" Trip yelled, moving the shield to block another shot.

Cutlass bit the top of the wax-like container off and threw the piece. It landed at a pirate's foot, releasing smoke from the small container as its chemicals mixed with oxygen.

"R-r-run!" Trip yelled, using the smoke diversion to seek cover. As he ran, he saw Erich lower into the Central Park Dome.

Erich launched several wires at the disguised pirates. But one guy was hidden behind a tree with his gun pointed at him.

"E-E-Erich!" Trip yelled to warn him.

Erich slung the pirates attached to the wires into the park's trees as he landed and ducked a shot from the hidden pirate, then launched a pulse wire to the guy's face. With a click of a button, Erich sent an electric current down the wire to shock the guy. Erich yanked him toward him, let the pirate pass by, and kicked him in the back to speed the process. The pirate's body wrapped around the wire and spun through spewing fountain water nearby.

With another pirate taken care of, Erich heard Trip yell and emerged from the smoke to try to find him.

"Ah, so you know him," a pirate said, having Trip in a headlock with a gun pointed at his temple. "Even better."

Erich stopped and then looked around to see Feit in the distance fighting pirates, and guards rushing to help. He watched a woman get shot and fall to her knees, yelling the name, "Timmy." He watched her child scream, running to her side. It was the lost kid Feit found. He could see Feit kill the pirate as the father rushed the kid away from his mother to escape, and the kid held tight to a toy visor. Erich's attention then focused back at Trip, who was held hostage by a man who seemed to be another ranked officer.

"What do you want?!" Erich said.

"Just to toy with you, is all," the pirate, Ferrous, said. His suit was black with chrome detailing, as well as an insignia Erich didn't recognize. He wore a bulky helmet with a tinted visor to keep his eyes from being seen.

"I thought you're supposed to take over the ship?"

Trip struggled, but the pirate kept the gun steady. "Just to toy is all, per orders," he said. "To toy with you, of course, Erich Botland."

Erich was silent for a second, wondering how he knew his name. "Let him go!" he demanded.

"You won't kill me," the pirate said. "And thus, you're only killing yourself."

Erich raised his palm in the air.

"Uhn, uhn, uhn," Ferrous said, jabbing Trip in the head some more. "I have magnetism as well."

"Wou-would you qu-qu-quit that!" Trip yelled. "Is th-that thing even clean?"

"Oh, aren't you scared!" Ferrous said sarcastically. "What's it take to get a good hostage these days!"

"I said let him go!" Erich demanded again as his wrist panel raised to reveal five pulse-wire tips.

"You're pathetic," Ferrous said. "You know as well as I do that this bullet travels faster than those wires of yours."

"Yeah, I know," Erich said with a smirk. "So look to your left."

Ferrous looked over to see a fist coming at him. The fist shattered his tinted visor and pounded him in the face.

The knuckles yanked back out, belonging to a one-armed, middle-aged man named Cutlass. Ferrous was knocked backward, firing randomly.

Erich's wire snatched the gun from Ferrous while another latched to his leg. When Ferrous hit the surface, Erich yanked the wire to drag him closer, then stepped on him and rolled him over for the wire to bind together.

"You should have taken the gun from him first," Erich said to Cutlass. "Someone could've gotten shot."

"Arr, only got one arm, me lad!" Cutlass reminded him, waving his stub.

They could hear Trip grunt and fall to his knees.

Erich looked over to see Trip with blood running from his arm. "Am-am … I OK?" Trip asked, panting, taking the pain.

"No!" Erich yelled and rushed to his aid. "I mean, you're just fine! We'll get you a doctor, OK?"

He didn't mean for his words to ring true. He was just warning Cutlass. Nobody was supposed to get shot, he thought.

Ferrous laughed while restrained.

"Good riddance!" he said.

His laugh was cut short by a knife in his throat.

"Sir Erich, I be truly sorry for my buccaneers fall," Cutlass said, snatching his knife from Ferrous' throat, his one arm shaking. Tears began to flow down his cheeks as he ran to Trip's side. "If there be anything I may do to save me hearty's life, I be willing!"

Trip grunted as Erich clinched his teeth. What was important was Trip at this moment, Erich thought. He reeled a wire from the top of his wrist and tied it around Trip's arm to block the flow of blood.

"It's a poisonous shell," Erich said, noticing the veins

of his arm changing colors. "Greg, you need to find a doctor fast! I'll do what I can to hold the poison off. Just find someone who can help—a doctor or something!"

Erich laid Trip on the floor as Trip clutched his arm in pain. He gasped out numbers as he counted to ease the pain. He tried not to think of the unsanitariness of the bullet wedged in his arm.

"Don't ye be going to Davy Jones' Locker, now!" Cutlass said to Trip, not wanting him to die.

"The-the-then find a d-d-doctor!" Trip yelled.

"Aye-sir!" Cutlass nodded, stumbling up and yelling for a medic.

Cutlass screamed for help as Feit and the Coronan guards finished securing the floor, eliminating all the pirates. The guards split up to identify the dead and injured citizens caught in line of fire as Feit rushed to meet with Cutlass.

"What's the matter?" Feit said, wondering how weird Cutlass looked with one arm, and ragged, smelly clothes, and an unwashed beard.

"Me buccaneer be hurt—shot in the arm!" Cutlass said in panic.

"You must calm yourself, sir. Now where is he?"

"He be over there!" he said, pointing behind him toward the Central Park.

"Where are the medics when you need them?" Feit said to himself as he glanced around him. "Don't fret; I'll get some help," he assured the crazed looking man. He reached in his pocket and pulled out a small device. He clicked it and a Nexas-screen image of an old man's face appeared. "Dr. Azmeck, are you in the area?" Feit asked, having gone on this trip at Azmeck's and Leroy Johnson's request.

"Ah, Feit, how's the travel for you?" the doctor asked.

"Someone got shot and is still alive. Are you near the shopping plaza?"

"Hm, why, yes, of course," Azmeck replied. "Couldn't stay stuck in the residential area for long, my boy. The populous seemed really frightened in there."

"Good, then meet us at the Central Park," he said and disconnected the link.

03

Feit watched over Trip as Erich gathered the tied-up pirates to incarcerate. Cutlass was the designated spotter. He paced back and forth, keeping an eye out for the doctor. It wasn't long before he saw a man wearing a white doctor's outfit approaching.

"Well blow me down—a doctor, are ye?" Cutlass yelled. "Me buccaneer be hurt!"

Dr. Azmeck rushed to a stop, holding his back, slightly slumped, and stared at the pirate-looking fella. "Why yes, I'm a doctor, but no MD," he said exquisitely.

"Me lad be this way!" Cutlass said, grabbing him with his one arm and tugging him along.

"I can't guarantee the service I'll provide, however," Azmeck said as Cutlass took him near the Central Park. They reached Trip, and Azmeck looked over his wound.

"Ah, I see," Azmeck nodded. "Well I have an emergency medical kit in my laboratory."

Trip began to drift out consciousness, so Cutlass shook Azmeck by the coat.

"Me buccaneer needs ye now!" Cutlass demanded.

"Calm down," Feit said. "He can teleport it."

Azmeck laid a pad on the damp floor and activated transportation. A medical kit soon appeared on the pad and Azmeck removed a utensil from it.

Trip woke up from the sight of it. "I-i-is it clean? It-it has to be clean!"

"Don't you worry," Azmeck assured him and put the device in his shoulder. He was going to touch the bullet and disintegrate it, but the bullet had already ejected somehow. Trip slightly grunted as Azmeck reached in his kit and removed a syringe.

"I-I hate needles. I-I hate needles!" Trip exclaimed, panicking.

Azmeck stuck the needle in him anyway. "Now calm down, son. The bullet released poison in your bloodstream, and we must eradicate the substance from your body lest you die."

Trip continued to grunt but calmed down. He was no longer sweating and could breathe normally. "Th-th-thanks," he said. His eyes started to roll back into his skull from the pain, but his panic was gone.

Azmeck nodded and looked over at Feit. "That wire tourniquet seemed to have saved his life."

"Well thank him, not me," Feit said, pointing at Erich, who approached.

Azmeck looked over his shoulder to see Erich dragging thousands of pounds behind him—more specifically a dozen knocked-out and tied-up pirates.

"Is he OK?" Erich asked.

"Don't worry, he'll be fine," Dr. Azmeck said, retiring his equipment and closing his medical kit.

"Thank you," Erich said. He then recognized the

doctor. "Wait a minute, aren't you Dr. Azmeck?"

"Why yes, indeed." Azmeck nodded, folding up his transportation pad, which unfortunately was only a one-way teleportation device due to its small size. "I am surprised there are still some youth who have heard of me."

"Well, yeah, my father. He studied your works. He was somewhat of a renowned biologist, to tell the truth."

Azmeck was curious. "And he is?"

"Dr. Durrick Botland," Erich replied. He lowered his head. "He's in a better place now."

"Ah, yes, Botland," Azmeck said. "Deceased, you say? My, my, what a loss of talent. You must be Erich."

Erich was startled for a second. "Well, yeah. I guess you do know him."

"My, my, how you have grown."

"Excuse me?"

"You were a baby the last I saw you," Azmeck said, stroking his gray beard. "Anywho, I apologize, but I must be going. I have plenty of work to do."

"Oh ... well, all right then," Erich said, feeling somewhat awkward. "Just be careful, though. There are probably some more pirates still on the ship."

"Not to worry about me, son," Azmeck assured. "I have Feit with me, you see."

Feit walked over to Azmeck's side and bowed at Erich to say goodbye. "It has been a pleasure to meet you, Erich."

"You, too," Erich replied.

Azmeck waved. "Feel free to stop by my lab any time, OK?"

"Sure thing," Erich said as Azmeck and Feit walked off.

Cutlass butted in. "What a great lad he be—healing me hearty friend."

Trip stood up, holding his arm, looking to the floor as Coronan guards arrived in a hovering platform vehicle. They jumped off and rushed to the still-knocked-out pirates to round them up.

"Yeah …" Erich said softly and then looked at Trip. "Glad you're OK now. You just gotta take it easy from now on." He moved his gaze to Cutlass. "Thanks."

"Arr!" Cutlass said, nodding.

"Now let's go back to the quarters," Erich said as he walked off, exercising his arm. He looked over his scorched and dented armor and used magnetism to pull out the bullet still wedged in his arm. It hurt but he bit back the yell as it popped out and landed in the palm of his hand.

They didn't get far when yet another boom echoed through the ship—the sound of a crash. Guards finished gathering the pirates and dead bodies as Erich overheard them talking of another attack—this one again at portside.

Erich smiled. "Cutlass, look after Trip for me. Or should I say the other way around. I've got some more fighting to do."

"Are ye sure?" Cutlass asked.

Erich looked over his shoulder. "Yeah, why not?" He then quickly ran off for yet another battle. *It's going to be a long day*, he thought.

Elsewhere on the Corona ship, Vecto stood in a hallway at portside. Energy zigzagged down the wall in a circuit-board fashion, reflecting blue off the dozens of lifeless pirates collapsed at Vecto's feet. The newly deceased had taken their last breath, literally, from the lack of air, as Vecto had smashed their visors and sucked the air from the room. Vecto stepped over the dead as air blasted from vents below his feet in response to the atmospheric conditions. It was followed by the swoosh sound of a door sliding open at the far end of the hall behind and the sucking sound of air. Guards rushed in but stopped on their heels and gawked at the carnage decorating the hall floors.

"This room is secure," Vecto told them. "No need to stay here."

In regulation, the guards scanned for his TAC to verify his ID. It wasn't of military class.

"Mr. Newman," one of the guards spoke first. "You must return to the residence for your safety."

One of the guards whispered to his comrade, "Looks like he doesn't need to," and motioned toward the dead pirates.

"I am fine," Vecto said and walked off.

"But we insist," the guard continued. "Your ID does not show you are trained in combat."

Vecto stopped. "I'm self-trained," he responded. He then glanced to his right through the thick windows and noticed the main pirate ship speeding beside the Corona, leaning in closer despite the heavy barrage of fire the Corona unleashed on it. Due to their near-light speed travel in the gravity well, the pirate ship looked blurred as it crashed into the Corona.

"Go back!" Vecto yelled, thrusting his arms out as the ship shook.

He waited as a bridge shot from the pirate ship, crashing through the hull just ahead. The breach caused suction but only for a moment before the bridge released foam to quickly seal the hole. A detachable door then jettisoned from the viaduct and a line of pirates rushed out. The Coronan guards immediately went into combat mode, tapping sections of the inside wall, which in turn slid barriers out for protection. They readied their guns and yelled for Vecto to run as the pirates released knockout gas in the air.

Vecto stayed standing, using a thin section of his invisible shield to block the back half of the hall from the gas, while at the same time sustaining his image of Robert Newman in a suit.

"I said leave!" Vecto yelled at the guards as the pirates fired at them.

The guards could see bullets crash in midair beside Vecto, baffled, not knowing there was a shield.

Vecto shot overhead. A thick safety divider suddenly crashed between them and blocked the guards from the action. It was a barricade designed to block off a breached hull—something Vecto had to force down to keep them out of the way.

The pirates ceased-fire, bewildered that Vecto was still standing.

The red-suited robot walked through smoke as his shield sucked carbon from the bodies in the room. Calmly, he grabbed bullets stuck to his shield and flicked them back at them. Pirates were struck in the head and chest with piercing bullets, joining their other dead comrades. For those remaining, Vecto snatched one of the pirate's guns and used the blunt of it to smash his helmet, then spun it into his companion's stomach and knocked the last pirate in the side of the head with it. He handed the gun back to its owner as the pirate collapsed to the floor. All were eliminated. But Vecto could detect more inside the bridge.

He stepped over bodies as a gravity wave vibrated across the ship. Gravity was lifted and bodies began to float. Yet coming from the bridge was another pirate. He stepped from the bridge, wearing magnetized boots to keep him on the surface. Vecto analyzed him as he took slow steps. It appeared he was a middle-aged pirate officer. His black, enhanced armor was splashed with green, bearing an insignia. He was brave enough to go without a helmet, revealing the many scars on his face as the few strands of blond hair adorning his head hovered in the air. In one hand was a double-bladed sword. In the other was a hand-held force field device, which created a barrier in front of most of his body.

Casket spun his two-sided blade in front of him as if a staff, clutching the center handle. "I'm not like those pawns," he said as he looked past the floating bodies to Vecto. "I am a superb fighter who has sent legions of men to their graves. With my Obitus, I will kill you!"

Casket spun the sword in the air and kicked a body at Vecto. He then propelled himself at Vecto with reverse magnetism as Vecto knocked the body aside. One of the blades of Obitus crashed into Vecto's head as Casket spun around and slammed the other end into Vecto's side. But there was no blood drawn accompanying the strikes. Casket stood in awe as his blades didn't even make the slightest cut. Barely a scratch.

"Ow," Vecto joked, grabbing the blade. "So you guys must be after me."

"Who *are* you!" Casket yelled, straining to yank his sword from his grip, amazed at the power of his suit.

Vecto brought the blade up and bent it by sucking its carbon bonds. "I'm the renegade robot, you see," he said. His fake human image then slowly faded to reveal his orb.

The pirate was speechless, letting his Obitus sword go as he leaped back, wading through the bodies.

"Now, what do you want with me?" Vecto asked.

The man was unresponsive as his boots magnetized to the floor and he kept his shield in front.

Vecto returned to his human image and flipped the sword around to point the other blade at him, using the bent end as a handle.

"I-I-I don't know what you're talking about! We're just here to raid the ship."

"Oh … my apologies then," Vecto said, thinking they were looking for him instead. He tossed the sword back at Casket. "I suggest you leave then."

Casket snatched it as Vecto walked over to a panel to open the sealed half of the hall. Vecto figured the guards were gone by now. The blockade lifted back into the ceiling, but a female stood before him, pointing her rifle at his chest.

Casket took the advantage to attack Vecto once more. He leaped and came down with his sword, striking Vecto's back. Once again, it had no effect. But more fearsome then Vecto was the stare from the woman's mechanical eye. The pirate's eyes bulged as the female quickly lifted her sniper rifle and blasted him between the eyes-close-range. The bullet grazed by Vecto's unresponsive head.

"Give it up, Vecto! I'm the one after you," she said as Casket's body floated back, leaving a trail of blood.

"So you listened through the wall," Vecto said. "And I bet you scanned through the barrier as well to see my orb, Accura."

"You remembered my name, huh?" Accura said, gliding back to make room for mobility as she kept her rifle pointed at his chest, her mechanical eye pinpointing the location of his orb.

"So what brings you on this voyage?" Vecto queried, not even bothering to attack.

"I planted spyware on Dr. Azmeck's balcony and overheard him say that he was going to load you on this ship. Only a fool would believe you were dead without presenting your orb," she said, referring to the battered body that Streamline fooled the police with.

"And these attackers?" Vecto asked, motioning to the bodies hovering around him.

"Have nothing to do with me," Accura said. "I work alone."

"Well then, how about—" Several disks and bombs launched toward them, cutting off his words. Vecto quickly snatched a disk inches from Accura's face and used his shield to block the bombs. The explosions ripped through the other half of the hall, dented the wall and cracked the thick windows of the hull. Accura quickly cartwheeled to the side while she sniped at the incoming pirates. She floated back against the wall behind a barrier as Vecto turned to face them.

Before he retaliated, the entranceway to the hall behind him opened and a figure floated through it in zero gravity. It was Erich, coming to fight the pirates. But he in turn was startled to find Rob instead.

"Rob?!" he said and then looked over to see a black, Japanese-looking female against the wall with her sniper rifle at the ready.

Accura motioned with her gun for him to take cover as several pirates rushed from the bridge, blazing bullets their way. Erich kicked himself to the wall panels for cover as Vecto zigzagged toward the enemies.

Vecto knocked several down until he reached the one

guarding the viaduct. He punched the guy in the face and knocked his gun in the air. As the guy's body flipped horizontally, Vecto then kneed him in the back and elbowed him in the chest, letting his limp body bounce off the ground. More pirates stood inside the bridge, waiting for him, and immediately fired.

Vecto grabbed the downed pirate's gun floating in the air and fired back, killing them as he approached, as light from the gun flashed across his body. They all fell to the floor dead, except one. The pirate was injured, yet managed to reach for a panel and clicked the hatch button.

A door from the bridge crashed on top of a body as the bridge broke away from the Corona's hull, retracting back into the enemy ship. It left a large hole in front of Vecto as air sucked out into space, followed by the whirlwind of dead bodies. But Vecto stood, locked to the floor by his shield as bodies slapped into him, flapping into space. He watched as Erich and Accura grabbed hold of handles on the wall, but he remained standing, watching them as the safety hatch overhead fell to save them, blocking him from their view once more.

Soon, the air settled, and gusts of oxygen burst from vents below. Erich floated in the bloodstained hall, upset he couldn't save Rob, as the gravity finally returned, forcing him to land on his back.

"I could have saved him …" Erich said to himself as he rolled over and pounded his fist on the ground.

"Don't worry about him," Accura said, not wanting to tell anyone he was really Vecto. Besides, the robot was her target, not someone else's to take the bounty. *Especially not this kid*, she thought. She knew well what kind of suit this guy wore. But why did he call Vecto 'Rob?' Was it the identity Vecto assumed?

"Come on; let's not dwell on it," Accura said, resting her sniper rifle on her shoulder, pleased that her earlier-broken legs had healed in just a few days. "There may be more pirates on board to round up."

Meanwhile, unbeknownst to Erich, Vecto was still alive, floating in space. He had ditched his human image and clung his orb to the hull of the ship. He rolled around for a bit among the exchange of firepower, analyzing the pirate ship still battling with the Corona. The bright blasts blurred by, distorted as all light trailed behind the ships due to their speed. It appeared every time the ship fired, it left an opening in its shield.

"I've had enough of this petty attack," Vecto muttered as his orb glowed. More blasts shuttered by in silence as all sound was lost in space. Vecto waited, figuring the seconds between each blast, distance, and speed. Two seconds and twenty-four milliseconds between each shot, 0.9034 gap, 4.2563 degrees, 98.6736 yards, 2,978 miles per hour. He quickly timed the attack and catapulted from the Corona's hull as if a cannon launched him toward the enemy ship.

A blast fired from the pirate ship, streaming past Vecto's orb as he zipped through the opening created for the blast. His circular body smashed into the enemy ship; it penetrated the hull and ripped into a dark room. Automatically, a barricade sealed the breach in the hull as the orb clanged on the floor and rolled to a lonely pirate's foot.

"Huh?" the pirate mumbled, apparently drunk, looking down at the orb rolling across the floor. "Is it a bomb?" he slurred, tilting his head, curious as to why it didn't blow up.

As if magic, the orb lifted in the air and hovered before

the pirate. The enemy blinked his eyes twice as a yellow translucent shield formed into a human body. But what startled him the most was that the image was him.

"Even worse …" Vecto's delayed response echoed in his ears.

Vecto raised his hand and began disintegrating his surroundings, including the pirate and his brief squeal. Junk parts from the room and pieces of walls smashed into Vecto's body as he sucked carbon from the room at maximum.

It not only affected the room, but the whole side of the ship. The pressure mounted, causing the ship's side to buckle inward. The force of the pressure immediately snapped the ship in two. One half of the pirate vessel crashed into the Corona, and the other half exploded. The first half then blew up, scattering fireless pieces in space as if they were smashed watermelons, but Vecto was somewhere … alive. His orb crashed onto the damaged hull of the Corona as brilliant colored pieces silently scraped by.

"The enemy combatant is destroyed, captain!" a female Coronan crewmember said. "But the portside shield is gone! And we've sustained severe damage to the hull."

"I see," Captain Tarcomed said, tipping his hat. "And how's the Graviton Flux holding up?"

"Let's see," the female continued, tapping screens of her holographic Nexas screen, then gasped. "Oh my, this is bad … the gravity well is unstable!"

"How bad?"

"Let's see. I estimate we have about … two minutes before it collapses," she said, her voice nearly breaking up.

"Just what I feared," Tarc said, stroking his salt-and-pepper beard. "The weight and velocity of the pirate ship along with ours, coupled with the force of the explosion, were too much for the well." The Captain contemplated briefly to muster a plan. "Give me shield status."

"Frontal shields are at ten percent," a male voice responded. "Dockside is at twenty-five and rear is at fifteen.

"Then pull us out of this worm hole," the captain ordered. "Commence procedures to return to real space at once!"

"But that force alone would tear our shields apart—and our ship!" the man responded.

"I am aware of the risks, lieutenant," Tarc assured him. "Does anyone have any better ideas?"

No one responded. It was impossible to normally exit a collapsing gravity well. That much they knew. So they had no choice but to do so by force, praying their shields would hold.

Captain Tarc nodded for the go-ahead. "Then start the countdown," he barked the order.

"Yes, captain," the crew said in unison.

It was a tough decision to make, Tarc thought—the only decision. He turned to the console and touched a holographic Nexas screen, exhaling. "Sarah, put all shield power to the stern and dockside. We're counting on you."

"Yes, sir, captain," the A.I. responded.

The captain lowered his head, wondering if they'd make it alive. "Brace for impact," he told the crew then held on to the arms of his chair until his knuckles turned white.

"Vecto ..." a soothing voice came from the hull of the ship. "Vecto?"

The Flummox Capacitor orb rolled along the hull of the Corona as Vecto heard A.I. Sarah's voice from the TAC attached to the side of him.

"I read you loud and clear, Sarah," Vecto responded. "Glad you found me."

"That's not hard to do with your drastic actions," Sarah responded, knowing it was him just by seeing his orb from the numerous cameras on the ship. "Now I'll have to cover up for you!" she joked.

"So what about the ship?" Vecto got to the point. "Are you going to make it?"

"Yes, but I need your help," the A.I. said in a worried tone.

"The Gravity Flux pipeline has become unstable and will soon collapse. So we're going to have to force our way from the gravity well. Only problem is, I don't have enough power to make an exit."

"So I guess you need me to stand at the stern, correct?" Vecto jokingly said, knowing he was likely right in his assessment.

"Well, yes," Sarah responded. "Assuming your shields are still functional."

"If my calculations are accurate," Vecto said, rolling toward the front of the ship, "then I should have enough carbon from the pirate ship to break through. I'll be spared with little if any power, however, but I estimate I have a ninety percent chance of succeeding."

"Well, that's better than our odds," Sarah said. "Then you'll help?"

"Already on the way," Vecto said. "Just remind me that I have a question for you when I get back."

"OK, but hurry," Sarah said, her voice fading as Vecto approached the stern. "Only a few … seconds remaining.

Take care!"

Static interference took over as Vecto rolled to the tip of the ship. The form of his yellow translucent body hunched up from the stern, looking up as if staring into space. He slowly raised one arm above him as if reaching for the stars. The bright-streaking walls of the gravity well zipped by as Vecto stood ready to take the impact.

He knew the force was going to be massive—something he hadn't experienced in a long time. But he was confident his trusty Force Field Shields would hold up. Vecto slammed his shielded foot into the hull of the ship and forced his other one in beside it for grip. All he could do now was wait as the shield from his hand expanded across the ship.

In seconds, the ship jolted and steered to the left. There was no more time for contemplation—only reaction. Vecto expanded his shield completely over the nose as the Corona jerked toward the side of the tunnel. In one massive impact, it collided with the wall, pounding Vecto's shield.

As if human, Vecto could feel the enormous pain from the hit, finding himself screaming from the collision. The wall scraped against his shield as if he were a human being dragged across a brick surface.

The scraping continued as Vecto took the pain. But as the crucial seconds passed, the ship finally dug a hole into the gravity well. Vecto's vision blurred as streaks of light tore by him as if thousands of needles traveled at the speed of light. Then with one final push, the ship broke through. It was as if it emerged from thin air; half of it was in real space as the other half pulled through. Frenzied asteroids flew by as the ship emerged from the hole at half the speed of light. But the ship kept going, and the rest of it finally escaped from the tunnel—a space-time contortion that was like traveling at hundreds of times the speed of light in seconds.

It was a relief to Vecto as he shrunk his shields and pulled his now-knee-deep legs from the ship. But he noticed the force had slung the Corona wildly in space, too dangerous in this asteroid field. Despite the ship's struggle to gain balance and slow down, Vecto knew he had to step in once more.

Yet before he could, his scanners picked up a fast approaching asteroid. He reached his hand out and braced as it collided with his shield.

It was a head-on collision, both Vecto and the asteroid traveling at astronomical speeds. In cyphen seconds, Vecto stood with a massive rock held back by his palm. The two forces made an abrupt stop, yet the impact was too much for Vecto. His shielded body slammed into the hull of the ship. The deathblow drained the last of his power and crushed his body between the ship and asteroid. It was a force thousands of times stronger than a nuclear blast—a force so grand that not even Vecto's shields could withstand.

The nose of the Corona formed a crater, and the asteroid shattered into billions of pieces. Meanwhile, Vecto's shields were now obsolete, deactivated. All there was left of him was his orb, unresponsive, floating in space as if garbage—spinning and tossing among debris.

"Vecto?" Sarah called out. "Vecto?"
Nothing but static.
"Vecto? Are you there?" she asked, using cameras from the damaged hull of the Corona to scan for Vecto's orb. But there was too much debris from the crumbled asteroid

to find him.

The ship was at a creep now, slowly spinning as Sarah continued her search for Vecto. But still, she couldn't find him.

"Come on, Vecto!" she said to his TAC, beginning to get flustered. "Stop fooling around and answer me, you metal head!"

But there was still no response. He couldn't have been destroyed, could he? Vecto had always seemed indestructible; he could survive anything. But he needed carbon, she reminded herself, and out in space, he was helpless without it.

"Vecto!" Her panicked scream echoed through the transmission.

"Well, captain, the shields took the blunt of the force," a female crewmember said, relieved. "Main damage is at portside, though, and we need to repair. But what's startling is how much shield power we have left."

"So what's the reading?" Tarc asked.

"Dockside is at five percent, but frontal shields are at ten."

"Ten?" the captain stuttered. "You mean point ten?"

"No, captain. It's the same as before in the gravity well. It hasn't changed."

"That's preposterous!" the captain snarled. "We saw it ourselves! The stern took most of the impact—even the asteroid."

"Well, captain, unless there's a glitch or an act from God, that's what the reading says," the female continued. "Sarah must have performed some miracle for this to happen."

"Hmm, quite peculiar," Captain Tarc said, stroking his

beard. He plumped back into his captain's chair as it contoured to his body. "At any rate, we're safe for now as long as we exit this asteroid field. Find the nearest planet that can bandage our hull and plot a course. We should be thankful we're alive."

"Yes, captain!" the crew said in unison.

The captain buried himself even farther in his chair, taking a sigh of relief. He then clicked a device on the temple of his head. "Congratulations, Sarah. You've done well." He paused to take another breath. "Now let's get out of this asteroid belt's orbit, shall we?"

04

"Vecto …" Sarah said through Vecto's com channel. "You need to ask me a question, remember?" She waited for an answer. "I'm listening, Vecto."

Each communication was the same—only one way. Vecto never replied. Even scanning the asteroid debris came up negative. It meant she couldn't find his orb or pick up any signals. And now the ship was slowly drifting away.

"Sarah," a voice said. It was Captain Tarc. "It seems we're in the Alpha Centauri system, which means planet Hodos should be nearby. Propel the ship in the same orbit as the asteroid field, and when we get close enough, contact the Magnatronians for permission to land and repair."

"Yes, Captain," Sarah said, dropping comlink. Gradually, they were leaving the site of the asteroid crash and there was still no sign of Vecto. She couldn't order a search because it would reveal his identity—besides, she couldn't even stop the ship without endangering the crew.

Although they were safe for the time being due to the vast distance between the asteroids, one of them could easily zip by and crash into them.

"Vecto, it's your last chance! Answer me!" Sarah desperately yelled through to his TAC. The ship began to move faster as the rubble receded in the distance with the stars. Sarah recalled the times she was the A.I. for Gyro's ship years ago. She remembered Vecto was less serious then, goofy at times for a robot. He liked her voice, he had said, and understood her. He was the one who assured her that she was not just a machine, that she had a life and a personally, like him.

"Goodbye," she said as the transmission went out of range from the site.

Meanwhile, in the residential zone of the Corona, Erich sluggishly walked to the wall at the right of his small quarters and clicked a button to release his bed. A metal panel slid out horizontally from the wall and locked in place, followed by the quick release of a compressed cushion. Erich slumped to the bed and melancholically detached panels from his suit, removing the upper half.

"Wh-wh-what's the matter?" Trip asked, sitting on his bed in pajamas across from Erich, his arm bandaged in a wrap. "I-I-I'm fine now. Just a scratch."

"Arr! The bunk I go!" Cutlass said, clicking a button on the wall to release a step-ladder to climb to his bed on top.

"W-would you be serious f-f-for a second!" Trip argued at Cutlass.

"Sorry mate!" Cutlass said, jumping on the bunk and dangling his feet below.

"Eww!" Trip closed his nose as Cutlass' feet passed in front of his face—without shoes. His socks smelled like they hadn't been washed in months, so Trip pulled out a detoxification spray from his pocket and drenched his feet with it.

"Heh, heh! That tickles, me buccaneer!" Cutlass laughed.

Trip wasn't laughing, though, and neither was Erich, which was even more disheartening.

"E-E-Erich? You OK?" Trip asked again.

Erich set another piece of armor plating on a small table squeezed between their beds and laid back into the bed cushion with his hands behind his head. "I saw Rob," he told them.

"R-re-really? Is he OK?" Trip inquired, wondering where he went.

Erich paused, looking at the ceiling at the small domes that lit up the room. "He didn't make it," Erich said, shaking his head. "He got sucked into space."

"Shiver me timbers!" Cutlass blurted. He frowned and took off his bandana, lowering it to his chest. "The poor lad."

"A-a-are you sure?" Trip asked Erich.

Erich took an extended breath, still disappointed in himself. "Yeah," he replied with a soft tone. "A hole was punched in the ship, and the safety hatch sealed him with it. And yet I couldn't do a thing to save him!" He punched the air in anger, looking at his battered arm.

"It be not yar fault, me hearty," Cutlass assured.

"Y-y-yeah," Trip agreed. "Don't g-ge-get yourself all depressed about it. You still have us."

"Yeah, I guess you're right," Erich said, trying to shake off the guilt and massaging the muscles in his soar arms. "Tomorrow will be another day. I need to count my blessings that you two survived and look onward. I'll train even harder, I'll get better, and I won't let the same thing happen to you guys!"

"Now that's the spirit!" Cutlass cheered.

"Y-y-you should g-get some sleep," Trip advised, lying in his bed. "I-I-It'll be better in the morning." He looked up at the bottom of Cutlass' bunk. "And y-y-you, Cutlass, get a bath, you rancid bigot!"

Elsewhere, near the rear of the Corona, an orb glowed through the inside of the hull. Metal melted as a black object burned through it, moving the liquefied metal behind to cool and seal the hole from space. The orb slowly popped out from the wall and fell, landing in a large waste disposal carrier.

"Detecting waste products," Vecto said to himself, "classified as organic." It meant he was aboard the ship. The last thing he remembered, his systems blacked out when he was struck by the asteroid and returned later when he slammed into a piece of debris. He recalled that he had no shields, not even his orb, but they flickered on when he hit the chunk of rock. Fortunately, he sucked enough carbon from it to propel himself toward the Corona as it was leaving.

"All systems check," Vecto said. "Operating at normal capacity." He slowly hovered in the air and scanned the room filled with crates of trash. The room had waste carriers, or twenty-foot-tall trash bins, lined against both sides of the wall and cranes that would magnetize metal from the trash and drop them into other bins for recycling. Vecto's orb rotated as he noticed trash being dumped into a waste carrier from a funnel above. A light went off indicating it was full, and the carrier began to roll across a rail system. It moved down the center aisle toward the rear as a gigantic door spiraled open to let it pass, closing behind. A whoosh of gas could be heard as the door opened back up, letting the trash bin proceed back to its respective place. Except the container was now empty, albeit gas particles fuming from it. A small crate also emerged, rolling to a center panel.

"Disintegration," Vecto noted. He then heard an elevator door chime at the front of the large room and saw a man wearing a dirty brown uniform pushing a hovering cart full of small crates in the room. Vecto quickly dropped himself back into the trash.

He could hear the cart hum to a stop, and the man moving crates murmured to himself.

"Hmm, got another one," the guy said. "Now where's my TAC."

It sounded like he fumbled through papers, then picked up the crate and put it on his cart. The man then slid the box, perhaps to align it with the others. Vecto could hear him whistle as he walked around the room, possibly to check the equipment. He soon stopped at the bin Vecto was in.

"Let's see ... now how do you work this gadget? Medium ... looks full."

Vecto quickly emitted a radio wave to distort the reading, not wanting to be taken to the disintegrator.

"Huh? Now it's empty?" the guy said to himself.

Vecto could hear him scratch his head. Then he heard a device at the side of the trash bin lower and the man stepped on what seemed to be a ladder. *He must be checking it out for himself!* Then he would surely send the waste carrier off!

The worker climbed the ladder and reached the top. He looked over the edge and covered his face as heat and gas rose from the trash bin.

"Man, I hate the smell of these things!" he said, covering his nose as a looked in the dark, foggy bin. It seemed empty to him. It must have just come from the disintegrator, he thought as he climbed back down the ladder.

Vecto was safe. He had sucked the carbon from the trash and turned the leftover matter into gas particles. But he still had to escape. He rolled to the top of the bin to see the worker push his cart back to the elevator, whistling away. The magnetic crane was approaching, and he had to get to the elevator.

The flat, dangling disc from the crane hovered above and activated its magnetic pulse. It snatched Vecto with the magnetic force, snapping the orb against the thick, circular plate. Just what Vecto wanted, actually. Despite the strong pull, Vecto could still roll. He moved up the crane as it hovered over the pile of metal remnants, using his shield to adhere to it. Soon, he was rolling upside down on the ceiling. He maneuvered around wires and lights on the roof toward the elevator. At last, he could see the crate below with the man waiting at the elevator doors. Slowly, Vecto hovered down from the ceiling. He had to be quiet.

The elevator door chimed and Vecto dropped to the crate.

"Huh?" The worker heard a clang and looked over his packages. He saw a box out of place and straightened it, then pushed the cart through the elevator doors.

It was quite warm in the elevator, the worker thought. He adjusted his collar as he waited for the elevator to reach the Energy Conversion floor.

Vecto was hiding, disguised as a crate, waiting for a chance to escape. He could detect an atmospheric rise in methane particles—but it was nothing to be concerned of. He waited as the elevator hummed to a stop and as the man pushed the cart down a hall. The worker swiped his TAC to open a door and pushed the cart inside to a stop.

"Got some energy from underground for ya!" the worker said as he walked over to greet another man.

This was Vecto's chance. He dropped his disguise to roll off the cart. The vast room seemed overly busy; it was some kind of energy processing plant. Vecto rolled by machinery and stopped near the office. He waited until he saw the door slide open. A heavyset man walked out of it with some sort of snack in his hand. Vecto quickly rolled through the door before it shut and formed his shield to look like the guy. No one noticed. He walked among the office to try to find a terminal. He had to tell Sarah he was OK. He lost his TAC in space and knew she'd probably be worried.

"Hey, Trevor!" a buff officer called out as he approached. "Thought you went on break? Did you adjust the pressure gauges?"

Vecto shook his head.

"What? Now don't be slack'n!" Officer Haggleworth sounded frustrated. "Come on! Hop to it, fatty! Or you won't be going on break!" He slapped him on the back to urge him forward and quickly retracted his hand, looking over his red palm as if he slapped too hard. "Ow ..." he murmured to himself as Vecto went to work.

Just beside the gauge was a terminal.

"Sarah? Can you hear me?" Vecto said into it.

"Vecto?" her bewildered voice came back. "Is that you?"

Vecto looked up at the ceiling where tiny cameras were. "I'm OK now, Sarah. No need to worry."

Sarah wanted to scream in joy, a unique humanistic trait of hers, but she restrained herself. "And why would I worry? I knew you'd make it back safe."

"Sure you did," Vecto said with a hint of sarcasm, knowing her programming better than she probably knew herself.

"You can ask me that question now," Sarah's sweet voice replied.

Vecto looked around him to see if anyone was watching. Still clear. "I'm seeking the coordinates of a planet called Zendora in the innerverse. Morphaal has returned, and I have heard he plans to arrogate that planet's energy."

"What! You mean Morphaal's back?"

"Affirmative, so it's very pertinent that I have the coordinates of that planet. Morphaal and Sable have already destroyed the A.S. base, and I cannot allow him to destroy any lives."

"Zendora?" Sarah repeated the word, though with her processing power, she already knew the answer. "I'm sorry, but I don't know."

Vecto paused. If Sarah, one of the most advanced star planners in the omniverse, didn't know where Zendora was, would he be able to locate it?

"You know the innerverse isn't charted," Sarah explained. "It's a bunch of dark matter and black space between our Central universe and the parallel ones. I'm amazed there could even be a planet out there."

"I see," Vecto said as Sarah continued to talk. He looked around him again, but this time he saw the real Trevor walk back through the door, taking a bite out of his veggie bar.

"Trevor!" the buff boss yelled at him. "I thought you

went to adjust the gauges!"

"But I thought you said I can go on break?"

"Not until you finish your station!" Officer Haggleworth yelled, pointing toward the back. His eyes bulged as he saw Trevor at a terminal and then looked behind him to see Trevor again behind him.

Vecto made a fake smile. "Well, Sarah, I must go!" he interrupted her and disconnected comlink.

"AN IMPOSTOR!" the officer yelled at the top of his lungs as veins popped out from his face and neck. "Seize him!" he ordered as he rushed to the wall to sound the alarm.

Vecto couldn't let them find out who he was, and he couldn't risk killing them. He casually walked toward the workers as they rushed to tackle him. Vecto stepped out of the way and tripped one of them up. The other sporadically swung his fists at him. Vecto dodged the fists, but grabbed one and twisted it. He accidentally broke his wrist, causing the worker to scream in pain and curse him. Vecto pushed his arm away and slightly pushed him in the chest. The worker slung across the room and smashed through a breakable glass wall.

"I apologize," Vecto said as the other came at him. The worker pulled out a stunner and shot Vecto with it. Vecto looked down at the current and shrugged, then snapped the gun out of his hand and crushed it. With a slow kick, Vecto sent the man flying across a desk, scattering reports and office supplies everywhere.

"Security alert!" the boss yelled into the intercom system as the alarm sounded. "Lock down all stations! The control room has been breached!"

Vecto, with the oversized body of Trevor, suddenly jumped in the air over a desk and landed in front of the real Trevor. The worker's jaw dropped, not believing he was seeing himself. His knees quaked as his hands shivered in fear. Even his snack dropped from his numb hand.

Vecto snatched the snack bar as it fell, and Trevor passed out, crashing to the floor.

"Bring the guards!" Haggleworth yelled, but there was no reply from anyone else. He was the last one left.

Vecto slowly turned around to look at him. "It's your turn, and it's inevitable." He slowly paced toward Haggleworth.

"Don't kill me! Don't kill me!" the supervisor pleaded, dropping to his knees. "Please, spare me!"

Vecto stepped in front of him and yanked him by his uniform's collar. "I detect that you're hungry. Allow me," Vecto said, shoving the deteriorating veggie snack in his mouth and tossing him across the room.

Haggleworth's bulky body crashed into a stack of containers, followed by the sound of a door swishing open. Two armored Coronan guards rushed in.

"Where's the intruder!" a guard said, snapping his gun around the room and settling it at Officer Haggleworth, who was lying on the ground, bruised.

"Mm, mm!" the boss' stuffed and muffled voice said. His hand trembled in the air as he pointed at Vecto, who was now disguised as a worker and was leaving through the door.

"Hey you!" the guards yelled. They ran through the entranceway, but the intruder disappeared.

"We'll do a search. Flag the right! Don't let anyone leave without being cleared, understand?" a guard ordered the other.

But Vecto was right next to them, in the guise of a crate. When they cleared the area, he slid across the floor, hiding behind machinery as he eventually made his way to a cart stacked with more energy crates on it. The gauges on them read empty.

"Hey, Drew!" a guard told a worker. "Sorry, but we gotta check your ID before you can pass. We've got a changeling trespasser around here.

Vecto noticed the worker was the guy who carried the crates up.

"Sure thing," Drew said as he lifted the last crate and put it on the cart. His hand stung, but he shook it off, then showed his TAC.

When he was all cleared, he left the room and pushed the liftcart down the hall to the elevator.

"I'm going up," a voice said behind him.

The worker turned around to see a middle-aged man with a goatee. "Sure thing." He took a better look. "Hey, aren't you that guy from TV?" he asked.

Vecto kept silent, wondering if he was busted.

"Um ... Robert! That's it. Robert Newman, isn't it?" he squealed in joy. "My name's Drew. I watch your liberty news show all the time!"

Vecto nodded as the elevator chimed.

"You're voice sounds different on TV though ..." he said slowly, but then his eyes brightened, and Vecto let out a sigh of relief. "Can I have your autograph?"

Vecto hesitated. He didn't even know this Robert Newman guy's signature.

"Wait, I thought I had my stylus here somewhere," the worker said, checking his pockets.

Luckily, he couldn't find one.

"Well here, you take this elevator then, Mr. Newman! I've gotta go down anyway, and I'm gonna need the space for the cart."

Vecto nodded and smiled as he stepped in the elevator, making a kind gesture with his hand to say thanks.

"I'll be watching your show!" the worker said with a big smile. "Nice to meet you!"

The elevator doors slammed shut. Finally, Vecto was free.

"Y-you know what's peculiar?" Trip asked Erich, who was now bundled in his covers in the other bunk.

"What?" Erich asked.

"Th-that bullet. It didn't really hurt all that much—when it hit me, I-I mean. And m-my body seemed to reject it."

"That's odd …" Erich pondered, gazing at the ceiling. "Maybe you got some superhero power, huh?" he joked.

"Y-y-yeah right!" Trip laughed.

The humorous tone briefly blocked out Cutlass' loud snore. But the quietness perhaps enticed the snore to get louder.

"Geez, I-I'd like to put that wretched sock of his up his mouth!" Trip said.

"Now let's not be too harsh," Erich said. "I'll let you borrow a squeaky clean one instead."

Trip made another slight laugh, but stopped when his arm stung with pain. "Hey," he said, looking over to Erich's bunk. "Th-thanks for all the help back there at the plaza."

"No prob. Let's get some sleep."

Erich circled his eyes across the ceiling, following the lines of blue energy supplying power to the dome lights. People had died today in disasters beyond his control. It reminded him of his days in bounty hunter school. He had taken this journey to get away from it all—the killing, the drama, the backstabbing. He wanted to find his own path in life, to discover his own identity. And he didn't want any more of his friends dead.

Three consecutive knocks echoed in the room.

"Huh?" Erich sat up and looked at Trip, who arched an eyebrow. "This late?" He settled his feet to the cold floor and cautiously walked to the door. A panel slid out from the wall and Erich activated the door's micro cameras. Standing at the door was ... "Rob?" he whispered in disbelief.

"Y-y-you mean?" Trip quickly sat up.

Erich clicked a button to open the sliding door and, behold, Robert Newman casually strolled in.

"I need a place to stay if you don't mind," Vecto said, a bit obtrusive.

"Rob!" Erich shouted. "Is it really you? But I thought you were dead!"

"In the flesh," Vecto said, amused by the irony as he stood by the bunk. "It appears my suit held up in space after all. And I was fortunate enough to find an open hatch to reenter the ship."

"G-g-glad you survived," Trip said.

Vecto scanned the sixteen-year-old kid and noticed his arm was shot by a bullet. "It's unfortunate you were shot," he said.

Trip looked at his bandaged arm. "Oh, yeah ... n-no-nothing to be terribly concerned about."

"Well, seeing that you made it alive, I guess you need your rest, huh?" Erich said, clicking for a bunk to align above his. A ladder with broken bars slid with it as Erich gestured.

"I am fine," Vecto said, standing by a wall.

"He m-may be afraid of heights like me," Trip suggested.

"Oh, well take the bottom bunk then," Erich offered. "Don't worry about it. I'll take the top bunk." Erich climbed the ladder and slumped across the upper bunk.

Cutlass' snore interfered.

"Should we wake him?" Erich asked Trip, guessing he might want to know Rob was alive.

"I-I'd rather hear his snore than his m-mouth," Trip coldly said.

Erich shrugged, then looked at Vecto. "So how'd you find us?" he asked curiously.

Vecto walked over to the bed and awkwardly sat down. He had no reason to sleep but knew he had to fit in.

"I found this place through the ship's database," Vecto responded. "I lost my TAC in space and needed a place to stay." They were true statements. He had indeed lost his TAC—although he didn't necessarily need a residence. He could have easily hid. However, for him to fit in with the human race, he had to study their ways. And what better way to do that than with Erich, Trip, and Cutlass.

"Oh, well, feel free to make yourself at home," Erich said. "We can get you a new TAC in the morning. But you know, I was wondering. Why were you over there fighting the pirates, anyway? Are you trained in some martial arts or something? You weren't that bad out there, you know?"

"I have done a bit of self-training in the past and seemed to have been caught up in the middle of the fight."

"Oh, s-so you're like Erich, huh?" Trip butted in the conversation. "Y-you should have seen him at the p-pl-plaza, kicking butt left and right!"

Vecto paused, looking at the pieces of Erich's suit on the nearby table. He had heard that Erich's father was head of the biological labs at a bounty hunter base called the Golen Station. Perhaps he was a hunter. It would explain the suit, Vecto speculated.

"You are a bounty hunter, aren't you?" Vecto asked. If so, he thought, it was even more reason to keep his identity secret.

"Well, not completely," Erich admitted.

Vecto paused as Cutlass' snore echoed across his shield.

"I was raised in bounty hunter school as a child," Erich explained. "It was all I knew, but I couldn't allow myself to kill anyone. So I was transferred to the creature's division for my test." He scratched his arm. "Up against merics … well, they're tentacle creatures on planet Arcous that steal energy. I know it sounds strange, but I couldn't kill them either."

"Why not?" Vecto questioned. "Wasn't that your job?"

Erich stared back at the ceiling. "It takes more skill to save a man than to kill him—the same for creatures, although I understand we need some for food. And well, sometimes, you just gotta follow your heart. If you've got enough conviction about something, then don't do it. There are always other jobs. So I left and boarded this ship."

Vecto thought about it for a moment. Was life that precious to him?

"I'm religious, too, you know?" Erich inputted. "It just goes against what I believe."

Trip shook his head. "S-so you believe in a mysterious h-hi-higher being that y-you can't see and have no proof that exists. I-It's just not logical."

"Logic is only human perception on how they perceive the universe," Erich said, staring at the lights. "Mankind has the choice to believe in God, even if proof smothers them."

"Th-the omniverse was created from the B-bi-big Bang," Trip explained. "Th-the particles formed planets, wh-wh-which sparked life and led to evolution."

"And who, or what, created that Big Bang?" Erich reasoned. "And how can this omniverse—not just one universe—be so perfect from just random occurrences? Where are the other universes that failed in the evolution of this universe? And how come God, when making the universe, couldn't have created evolution?"

"Y-y-you cannot prove there's a god," Trip argued.

"Neither can you disprove it."

Vecto remained silent, observing their religious quarrel. It seemed to be a sensitive subject to these humans.

Erich continued. "Look—no hard feelings. I respect your views. It's just something I personally believe is true. The universes are just so massive and complex that there has to have been some divine touch to make it all happen."

"May I interject?" Vecto asked.

"Sure," Erich said.

"I believe Erich is correct in his assessment," Vecto said, "that out of infinite possibilities, the omniverse is at perfection. The odds for this are overwhelming and even the mightiest machine will never know the truth, as they are programmed from the knowledge of man. However, on the other hand, if there is a god, then how does he exist as we do—assuming time is straight, which may not be the case. There are simply too many mysteries that not even man is capable of understanding."

"That's what makes us human," Erich added, "finding the truth. People seem to just follow what everyone else says rather than deciding for themselves. But we each have to make up our own minds."

Vecto paused. "Indeed. Mankind is swayed too easily.

Do they not develop a sense of probity for themselves? Or are they bound by their own manipulations?"

"I'd say yes and yes, but then again, doesn't that define man?" Erich replied with a smirk.

"OK, w-we-well it's getting late," Trip mentioned, alluding to how he was tired yet also trying to change the subject.

"Erich pulled covers over him and waited as it contoured to his body and warmed. "Yeah, I guess we ought'a get some sleep. Another big day tomorrow."

Trip snuggled in his covers. "G-goodnight then," he said.

"Goodnight, Trip," Erich said. "You too, Rob. No tellin' when we'll stop at Hodos."

Vecto paused. Hodos, as in Gyro's homeworld? He quickly reviewed star data from when he was in space. The analysis affirmed it. They were in the Alpha Centauri System and were probably going to stop for repairs. At least he could visit Gyro's gravesite, he thought, but he no longer had Gyro's cross. He lay back in the bed and closed his eyes—although he could still see around him.

Trip found it curious that Rob was wearing his suit to bed. He dismissed the thought as his covers warmed. But just as his eyelids drooped, he heard Cutlass' obnoxious snore!

"C-cut-cutlass!!" Trip yelled, astonished the pirate-wannabe could sleep through all the talking.

05

"R-Ro-Rob?" Trip woke up early in the morning, realizing that Rob's bed was empty and that the cushion was no longer there. "Hey, Erich," he called out. He rubbed his eyes and sat up, shaking his head to wake up. Erich didn't respond; he must have still been asleep. He blinked and looked at the table between the bunk beds. Erich's suit was missing.

"Erich?" he said again and stepped from the bed, sliding slippers on his feet, not wanting to touch the nasty floor. He walked over to Erich's bunk and climbed the ladder with a handkerchief. As he peeked his head over the top bunk, he saw he wasn't there. They must have gone to get breakfast, he thought.

Trip climbed back down the ladder. Cutlass was still snoring. He simply shook his head this time and left to take a particle shower.

"Attention. We are approaching planet Hodos in the Alpha Centauri system," Sarah's voice said over the intercom. "We will land shortly to undergo repairs. Please remain on this ship at all times. Only authorized individuals will be granted access to leave this ship."

It was now 7 a.m., Earth-standard time. Vecto stood at the end of a lounge next to a virtual arcade room, gazing at the panoramic view of space from the ship's window. He saw planet Hodos suspended in space. It was a mostly light blue planet with dark patches, home to many of the Magnatronians—and, of course, home to his friend Gyro, where his wife, Charisma, still resided. Vecto made a point to visit Charisma. Although she was an Exodite—longtime enemies to the Magnatronians—she happened to be Gyro's wife, the only reason the Magnatronians respected her.

"Beautiful view, isn't it?" Erich's voice echoed as he approached.

"Yeah," Vecto replied.

"Wish we could roam the planet while they make repairs."

"There's not much to look at," Vecto answered. "The Magnatronians are bred for war. Plus they don't get along too well with the Acaterran government. I'm surprised they're letting us land."

"You must have been there before," Erich gathered.

"I had a friend who grew up on this planet. I plan to visit his gravesite to pay my respects."

"Well, good luck on getting a pass," Erich said. "Sorry you lost a friend, though. I know how it feels." He leaned against the window seal to get a better view of space. "That reminds me. You still gotta get a new TAC, you know? Mind if I come along?"

"I'll be fine," Vecto said, still staring out the windowpane.

"Well, want to join me for breakfast then?"

Vecto turned around and walked off. "Maybe another day."

Erich was worried about his abruptness. "All right, but take care," he said as he leaned his back on the window sill. "You're welcome to stay at our quarters."

"Thanks," Vecto acknowledged, disappearing in the crowd.

With a soft touchdown, the Corona ship rested on the sparsely grassed, white-and-black patched ground of planet Hodos. Coronan guards blocked the exit as only ranked officers were allowed to leave. Dr. Azmeck walked by uniformed guards with Feit, headed for the robotic storage bay to retrieve Vecto's orb.

"Are you sure you want to do this?" Feit asked.

"Ah, yes, I will need his orb for my study," Azmeck nodded. "It's just speculation, but I believe his system may be ternary, having positive, negative, and neutral base coding instead of binary system machines typically use. Assuming that's the case, if I can link that programming to the logos compounds hagios, kakos, and artios, perhaps I can communicate directly to his system to find the cause to his dementia."

Feit tipped his head to the side.

"The fundamental properties of thought," Azmeck explained. "Good, bad, and undecided. Some speculate those properties make up the subatomic particles quark, leptons, and force carriers."

Feit tilted his head even more.

"Dinishmen technology already exists that allows people to insert their thoughts in other people's minds," Azmeck got to the point. "And the conduit is a ternary machine. So if Vecto is trit-based ... voila, problem solved.

We can communicate to him via thought and may be able to find what data is corrupted."

"If you say so," Feit replied. "You're the scientist."

The two were granted access to the storage room and walked past rows of robots. Something was different. Feit noticed an entire section of these manufactured machines were missing, with pieces of scrap metal adorning the floor as if it was a clearing patch in the midst of a forest. He suspected what happened but kept quiet as they made their way to Azmeck's clucky robot—supposedly encompassing Vecto's orb. Yet when they approached the machine, Azmeck noticed its chest was split open—with Vecto's orb missing.

"Holy Rama!" Azmeck yelled, stumbling back. His robot, Mike, was still deactivated, its head lowered—and no sign of Vecto. "This is catastrophic! Oh my, oh my, oh my, what are we to do? What if he's on another killing spree?"

Feit was calm as he looked inside the robot and studied it. "I doubt that," Feit said. "It seems the metal has had quite the time to reform. I suspect Vecto freed himself yesterday, and since we haven't heard of any murderous killing spree, I assume he's staying low, undetected."

"My word! Did you bring the energy capsules in case?" Azmeck asked.

Feit reached into a small pouch to his side and showed four energy shells. They were Leroy's energy—the same substance he gave to Streamline to use against Vecto if needed. And it seemed to have paid off. He snapped one of the shells into the blunt end of a small gun and returned it to his pouch.

"Indeed, I am so grateful you obliged to come on this trip. I alone cannot handle Vecto," Azmeck noted.

"Well it was at my master's request," Feit pointed out. "So thank him. He wanted me to join you as part of my training, I assume. He always tends to give me odd tasks …"

"Ah, I see," Azmeck said then contemplated for a second. "Hmm … considering Vecto has escaped and we so happen to land on Hodos, Gyro's homeworld, Vecto will most likely attempt to visit Gyro's grave."

"So we'll find him there, then. I'm ready when you are."

"Indeed," Azmeck said with a slight nod and stroke of his white beard. "Follow me."

"Ahem!" a voice echoed.

Azmeck and Feit turned around to see what appeared to be a guard approaching.

"This area is restricted for civilians," the silhouetted figure said as he approached. "You must come with me."

"But we have clearance," Azmeck reasoned. "Would you like to see my TAC?"

"I have orders to retrieve you," the man continued and grabbed his arm. "There must have been an error in granting you access."

Azmeck pulled away, feeling a sting from his grip. But when he turned to talk to Feit, the fighter had his chi gun pointed at the guard's head.

"Stay back, Azmeck," Feit ordered, holding the gun steady.

"My word! What do you think you're doing?"

"He's not a Coronan guard."

Azmeck looked at the figure and glanced at his arm.

"And neither is he human," Feit added, keeping a close eye on the figure.

Azmeck looked back at the uniformed man. "By golly!

It's Vecto, isn't it?"

The man smirked and looked at Feit. "Quite observant, Feit, but I'm not here for retaliation," Vecto said, keeping his disguise in case someone passed by.

"I could tell it was you when I couldn't sense any chi," Feit said, peering over the gun's barrel. "But how do I know you're not lying?"

"Trust me," Vecto replied. "I am not as destructive as I have been. And I was never deaf while in locked stasis, so I understand Azmeck's efforts to redeem me. However, I do not have any malfunctioned programming and will no longer need assistance."

"So then why did you escape, and why are you here?" Feit questioned, stepping back to keep the gun from arm's length.

"Immobile confinement for so long can only lead to further madness," Vecto retorted. "Besides, I came to retrieve Azmeck in order to speak in private—away from you, that is—to reveal who I am, but I no longer need to do that, now do I? So please, do put away that gun, for all it takes is a touch from my shields and a gun it will be no longer."

"He's right, Feit," Azmeck agreed. "If Vecto was still mad, we wouldn't be standing."

"The past is what it is," Vecto continued. "I am aware you gave Streamline those energy shells on behalf of Leroy due to my inconsistencies. But you will no longer need them." Vecto glanced away and turned around. "If you use them, however, I will not hesitate to kill you." He began to walk off. "Good day, sir."

"You obviously underestimate me," Feit said but slowly lowered his gun. "If you slip up, I have no qualms in using force."

"Very well, then," Vecto's voice became more distant. "Azmeck, you may come along if you wish. You already know where I am going. I'll meet you at the loading bay."

"Ah, Gyro, poor lad," Azmeck said, knowing Vecto was going to visit his grave.

"You're not actually going along with that crazed machine, are you?" Feit whispered, quite loudly, to Azmeck.

"I trust he is back to normal," Dr. Azmeck said. "Don't fret; Vecto would never kill me, and I have my locater if you must assist."

"It's not wise," Feit warned.

"I can take care of myself. Just watch my lab while I'm gone, would you?" Azmeck asked as he shuffled away.

Feit shook his head and rested his hands together behind his back. "I didn't come here for a babysitting mission," he murmured to himself, hoping he'd get to fight Vecto, the one being capable of standing his own against his master Leroy. He was going to keep watch on Vecto, anyway.

As hours passed, Vecto managed to successfully bypass the guards using a little diversion and disguise techniques—with the help of Dr. Azmeck. The two traveled on the cold, black, soot-like mud of planet Hodos. At least they were near the equator where there was little ice. Dust particles swirled in the wind as they eventually came to the entrance of a nearby military base and were greeted by a dozen pulse-rifles in firing pose.

"Military personnel only," a Magnatronian guard in black, standard armor stated while in crisp military stance.

"Excuse us," Vecto said, disguised as Robert Newman. "I have come here to request travel arrangements to visit a friend."

"Sorry, we ain't doin' taxi service," a buffer soldier said, standing firm in front of the large docking bay doors while taking a puff from his cigar device.

"We have come to visit Charisma, the widow of Gyro," Vecto continued, looking at the guns as Azmeck stepped away.

They were unresponsive until one soldier spoke up. "How do you know Gyro?" he asked, his face hidden by his body armor's helmet.

"I served under A44G," Vecto simply replied.

Silence again bestowed them as the soldier with a cigar slowly removed it from his lips and approached Vecto, looking him over.

"Gyro's Alpha 44 battalion was wiped out two decades ago," Weston spoke up.

"You forget that one member survived who fateful trip to Cardell. So I request to be taken aboard a liftcopter."

"Only a robot unit member survived that mission, not the likes of you, Terran." He pressed his cigar against Vecto's body, but it didn't burn him in the slightest—instead, the cigar burned up.

Vecto was getting impatient. He grabbed the soldier's arm and twisted it.

The soldier quickly stabbed Vecto's shield with a knife and took back his arm, but Vecto punched him in the gut. The soldier's nanobite suit had a temporary, form-fitting shield that protected him, but the Magnatronian still slid.

Vecto dropped his shield's disguise to reveal his orb floating in the air.

"Enemy combatant!" a soldier yelled as he abruptly exchanged fire.

Vecto's shield took the pulse beams head on. The

conversation didn't go the way he expected. He reached out with his invisible hand. The outer shield sucked in and quickly popped out, blasting a current of air at the soldier to knock him to the wall.

They were ready for the offensive, against what appeared to be a motionless orb, when they saw someone approaching.

"Attention!" a stern voice yelled. A man in a high-ranking officer's armor, white in color, approached them as the Magnatronians immediately backed away and took position with feet together and hands saluted.

"I apologize for their rash behavior—attacking without orders," the officer said to Vecto and Azmeck, who was now yards away from the action. "You speak of Gyro and A44G. What's your name and number, soldier?"

Vecto returned his disguise and stood straight. "Vecto Botland, sir. Number 52224712. Requesting travel to the Ondrea sector. Good to see you again, Commander Keefe."

The fifty-year-old officer gave a slight laugh. "Ah, Vecto Botland, the one true Terran robot we actually like. Well its admiral now, soldier, so you'd better get used to it. Been quite some years, hasn't it? Heard you got into some ruffles on Acaterra. I assume you're well?"

"Affirmative," Vecto said nodding.

"Good! Then let's prepare you a copter," Admiral Keefe said. "Any friend of Gyro's is a friend of ours."

"Requesting a guest to accompany me," Vecto stated, pointing at Azmeck.

"Indeed," Azmeck said, "If it is not too much trouble, that is. I am Dr. Az—"

"I am fully aware who you are, Dr. Azmeck. I will personally see to it that you can come aboard. Just hope you have a strong stomach," he said with a laugh. But despite his eased demeanor, his dark gray face looked worn from decades of combat. The admiral's sharp gaze looked into the eyes of a nearby soldier. "Open these bay doors and prepare the Etta for flight!"

"Yes sir!" the soldier replied, then made commands through comlink in his helmet.

"And you two," the admiral looked at the soldiers who attacked Vecto without orders. "Give me five hundred. On the double!"

"Yes sir!" they both said. They immediately did one-arm handstands and did pushups using one index finger.

Admiral Keefe then looked back at Vecto as the massive bay doors began to slide open behind him. "Come with me. We've got lots of catching up to do, don't we?"

Soon, Vecto and Azmeck were riding on a Class C Magnatronian Battlecopter. It wasn't any of the latest models so it lacked the newer weapons and modifications. But what stood out the most were the torn landing gear and wide-open space.

"Don't worry, this baby can hold its own!" Admiral Keefe yelled through the wind. He came along to personally see to it that Vecto made it to Charisma's home.

The copter zoomed over black domes used during wars to protect residences. It was a battlefield site, like much of this war planet. Vecto was standing in the center of the copter, unfazed, as a couple of soldiers at the edge simply held on to a bar overhead. Azmeck, though, was strapped in a seat, gazing out the open side of the copter at the wasteland.

"Upset stomach, yet?" Keefe yelled toward Dr. Azmeck.

"It's been a smooth ride so far," Azmeck yelled back.

"My nephew, Phantom, was quite the pilot, so I've had my share of fast flying."

"Good!" Keefe said and turned to the pilot. "Then let's have a little training exercise, shall we?"

"Roger that, admiral!" the pilot said with a smirk, yanking at the controls to do a barrel roll.

Azmeck's eyes widened as the copter spun and did a nosedive. The soldiers laughed as the copter free-fell then swooped over some trees and shot ammo at imaginary targets.

"Yehaw!" one of the soldiers blurted out as branches and leaves scraped by the ship before it soared over a cliff. "Let's make it lively, boys!" he yelled as Vecto remained calm, wondering what they had planned.

The wind shook the soldier back and forth as he put his helmet on and clicked a button. Sliding from a storage space beside Azmeck were three missiles the size of the soldiers themselves.

"Good gracious!" Azmeck was startled. "It isn't necessary to be bombing the planet!"

"Oh, we ain't gonna bomb the planet, Gramps," the other soldier explained. "We're gonna launch it back at us!"

"What!?" Azmeck yelled.

"Bombs away, boys!" The soldier grabbed hold of a missile and dropped out of the ship, followed by the others.

"Are they mad!?" Azmeck yelled at Keefe.

"Ah, don't worry!" Keefe replied. "We've only been hit once!"

Azmeck leaned over to see the missiles that the soldiers rode on activate boosters. In a flash, the men were sent flying by the battlecopter.

"Open fire!" Keefe ordered.

Azmeck grabbed hold of his seat as bullets sprayed at the three soldiers. One of the missiles was snagged so the soldier bailed out, spinning himself upside down and free falling from the projectile as it exploded. The others guided the missiles in a 180-degree turn.

"Quite the risk takers, as usual," Vecto calmly said in observance as the two missiles headed straight for them.

"Activate shields!" Keefe commanded.

One of the soldiers pushed himself off the missile, letting it continue.

"Roger," the pilot said as he activated shields and did a barrel roll out of the way.

The other warrior leapt off his missile, kicking it toward the copter.

"You need to shake it!" Keefe yelled as they rolled but the missile struck their shields.

Dr. Azmeck yelled as the copter shook from the blow, but it wasn't over yet. The last soldier who jumped smashed into the copter's cockpit windshield and lunged a fist through it.

"Get that enemy off this copter!" Keefe yelled as he took out a knife and stabbed his subordinate in the hand.

The pilot quickly reversed the copter's spin and made a nosedive. The soldier was still hanging on, his body being slung in the air until finally he lost grip and was tossed in the air.

Azmeck's yells persisted as the copter swooped back up and glided in the air, back to normal flight.

Vecto shook his head as he watched the last soldier plummet to the ground without a parachute, smacking the ground hard, creating a crater in the surface.

"As you see," Admiral Keefe explained, "these men are

equipped with top-of-the-notch technology, based on Dinishmen design. They're equipped with hybrid warpmetal-nanotech armored suits. The armor is self-repairing and can form a shock absorbed, interlocked coating of nanomachines to withstand heavy impact. They're also equipped with an AI companion system as an onboard battle computer, and for weapons, they're equipped with a reverse-linear accelerated rifle system, a phase-rail energy module, an omni-directional mass discharge system, as well as other battle configurations. Impressed yet?"

"Not really," Vecto said as he looked out at the horizon as they entered the Ondrea sector.

"Ah, figures," Admiral Keefe said as the cockpit glass began reforming. He then looked at Dr. Azmeck. "Well, it looks like you have a tough stomach after all!"

Azmeck shook his head and leaned forward in his seat. "I've been through much worse flying, but the live combat attacks from your men were quite unexpected."

Keefe smiled. "Well, this is it. Her place is comin' up. It's not often you'd have an Exodite like her living on this planet. If it wasn't for her being Gyro's wife, she'd be—"

"I'm getting off here," Vecto interrupted.

"OK, want me to land?" the admiral yelled through the wind.

"I'm going alone," Vecto said, stepping to the edge of the chopper. "Take Azmeck back to the base," he added, then jumped off.

"Hey! I thought I was coming along!" Azmeck yelled at Vecto's falling body.

Vecto was free falling like the Magnatronians had, except he deactivated his disguise and consisted only as an orb. The Flummox Capacitor whistled through the light blue sky as it crashed to the black surface, making a small crater.

Once again, he activated his disguise and slowly rose from a knee amidst the dirt swishing around his body. He needed some more carbon while he was at it, too, he thought. The black dirt stuck to his shield, and below him, another crater formed as he sucked carbon from his surroundings. Now to see Charisma. He could see her abode up the hill—a green dome in the middle of nowhere. He wondered how she would take to his visit.

Charisma was awakened by a buzz. Her sleeping pod depressurized, and the shield disappeared. Slowly, she sat up, groggy, wiping her eyes in an attempt to see. Her green eyes adjusted so she could glance at the time. It was ten o'clock. *Who's going to visit me this early?* she thought. She adjusted her nightgown to form into some decent clothes and brushed her fingers through her long black hair. It was a little mangy, but it had to do. She then grabbed her gun and attached its nozzle, in which two shield panels fanned out like two sides of a triangle. With a sigh, she stepped on a circular lift platform to take her to the surface.

Vecto waited at the edge of the dome as Charisma rose to the top level. Although the dome was tinted, he could see she was, as always, prepared for a fight.

"State your name and business," she said through the intercom, pointing her gun, still within the safety of the shield.

"It's Vecto."

Charisma paused to look at the human figure. "Prove it."

Vecto scaled back his disguise at his chest to reveal his orb.

Charisma laughed, then fired her gun. The bullet phased through the dome and struck Vecto. But Vecto caught the projectile and peered at it between his finger and thumb as it disintegrated into dust.

"Only Vecto sucks carbon," Charisma said with a smirk. "So what took you so long to visit?" she scolded him, lowering the gun.

"Didn't know you'd miss me," Vecto said, returning to the image of a red-suited figure. "I thought I'd check on you since I was in the area."

"Well let me know ahead of time next time," Charisma said as she tapped a panel a few times to deactivate the dome shield. "I'm not particularly dressed for company, you know."

"It's not like I particularly care," Vecto said, walking down a few steps to the center circle.

"I take that as an insult," Charisma said with a smirk as gusts of wind sloshed her hair around. "Come on," she motioned for him to step on the elevator platform. "We can talk inside."

They had a vibrant conversation about Vecto's psychosis, about Gyro, about the separation of the Alpha Squad. It had been only a few weeks since they last met, and Vecto and Charisma already had plenty to discuss.

"Staying out of trouble now, aren't you?" Charisma asked as she took a sip of drink.

"In a way," Vecto responded, watching a slide of pictures glide across the wall. They were mostly of Gyro. "I apologize I couldn't save Gyro," Vecto said. "I know you miss him. If there is anything I can do to assist …"

Charisma shook her head. "No. Just be yourself. That's what Gyro would've wanted."

Vecto watched the slide as a picture of him and Gyro

scrolled by. "I've heard Morphaal's back," he informed her. "When I find him, he'll pay for Gyro's death."

She shook her head again. "It wasn't Morphaal's doing this time, Vecto. It was D'urjin Tellal's, and he's already dead. If you're going to go after Morphaal, do it because of the other crimes he committed."

"I disagree. Morphaal was responsible for the Super Soldier project and made Tellal who he was, thereby being accountable for Gyro's death. He deserves—"

"Vecto!" Charisma raised her voice. "Gyro's death has already been avenged. It's time to move on and accept that he's not coming back this time."

Vecto kept silent. For her to move on must have been a daunting task, perhaps to cover up the pain. But why should he? He lacked such emotions.

"Besides," Charisma said, softly touching a picture of Gyro on the wall, "his legacy is not dead. It will be reborn."

"What do you mean?" Vecto questioned, although he gathered what she meant.

"I'm pregnant, Vecto. With Gyro's child."

Vecto nodded. "I know."

"Huh?" Charisma cocked an eyebrow.

"According to preliminary bioscans, I detected a fetus within your womb."

"Yeah, I bet you scanned me," Charisma said, crossing her arms.

"But the likelihood of it being Gyro's child seems improbable. Gyro was incapable of reproducing."

Charisma cut him an evil stare. "Why's it all about the technicalities? We did a genetic implant on our honeymoon. We were planning on settling down until he was called off to battle. He wasn't supposed to fight anymore—had given up the A.S. but couldn't see you guys suffer without him there to help." She lowered her head in thought. "I can pin the blame for his death on all sorts of things, but it doesn't solve the problem. Gyro gave his life because deep down, he cared."

"He saved my existence for reasons I cannot comprehend."

"And left me behind," she said with a chuckle. "That selfish hog!"

Vecto was already familiar with her demented humor. He decided to make his response light. "By the way, congratulations on the pregnancy, I suppose."

"Thanks," Charisma said as she grabbed a hologram picture from the wall and brought it closer. It was a picture of their wedding. "You know, if it's a boy, I'll call him Gyro Jr. If it's a girl, I'll call her Chasity."

"Gyro would have been delighted to have a son named after him."

Charisma stared up at Vecto's human image. "You don't have to lie, Vecto. He would have had a fit."

"I suppose."

"Well you'd better get going if you want to visit the gravesite," Charisma said, sitting down in her hovering chair. "The wind storms usually blow through in the afternoon."

"Very well then," Vecto said. "It has been good seeing you."

"You too, Vecto. You too."

06

Gyro's gravesite was halfway shadowed by an awning tree indigenous to planet Hodos. Its massive intertwining branches and five-foot-long leaves darkened half of Vecto's image as he knelt at Gyro's newly installed headstone. Images of Gyro and his friends scrolled across the tombstone as Vecto watched. He slid a hologram over to play the video he made. They were Vecto's memory logs.

"Come on, Vecto," Gyro said, looking at the screen. "Have some fun for a change, will ya?"

"I have no need for such pleasantries," Vecto's recorded voice responded.

"You take your bubble car and I'll drive the bike," Gyro said as he jumped on his liftcycle.

"A chase is not necessary," Vecto replied. "The chances you will win are slim at best."

"Never know till you try." Gyro laughed. "Guess I get the head start!" he yelled as he revved the cycle and catapulted off.

The screen shook as Vecto turned to look at his V-Extreme. It jumbled as Vecto jumped in his vehicle and started its magnetic-powered engine. "He asked for it," the voice of Vecto said as his robotic hand reached out to close the cockpit.

The video faded but another took its place. This time Gyro stood on the roof of Vic's lab on planet Cubix, looking at the nearby glowing city at night.

"You can't find a view like this on Hodos," Gyro commented, leaning against a small transmitter tower. "Such raw emotion and beauty."

"It means nothing to me," Vecto responded. "For me, life is existence. For you, life is emotion. That bridge cannot be broken."

"Then why fight, why save people if you have no emotions?" Gyro quipped. "Battles are forged through passion."

"Mankind knows not their destruction. For that reason, I must protect them."

"And isn't that emotion? Defending the defenseless?"

"For every man Morphaal kills, that's one more who pleases him. I seek to give him ultimate displeasure."

Gyro looked at him. "You sure do have some twisted logic," he said with a laugh. "Someday, Morphaal will be dead for good, then you'll have no reason to protect people."

"I'll do it for you, then."

Yet another video clip played.

"Ah, you're awake. I see my reprogramming works," Gyro said as he fiddled with Vecto's shoulder not in view. "How's your eyesight?"

The screen moved left to right as Vecto glanced around. He could see Gyro's grayish-black skin. "With some modifications, it will do."

"You took a pretty bad beating, you know? Had to fix a lot of you—basically gave you a new body."

"I assume you defeated Morphaal."

"Yeah, he won't be coming back now," Gyro said as he worked on Vecto's arm. "I couldn't figure out how to make your pieces hover, so I made you one unit. Hope you don't mind ... and Vecto, thanks for the sacrifice."

"The physical inconveniences are no problem. I am grateful for your services. I understand what it means to be moral now, thanks to you."

"And how so?"

"For me to understand myself, I must first analyze my morality and determine the appropriate outcome of my endeavors. The outcome of you dying would be unbearable."

"So you're finally understanding emotions, huh?' Gyro said with a smirk. "Don't worry, I'm not going anywhere."

The video stopped.

Vecto lowered his head at Gyro's grave. *How ironic we would share the same fates*, he thought. He glanced down at a Biblical verse inscribed in the headstone. It was Ecclesiastes 9:10, which read, "Whatsoever thy hand findeth to do, do it with thy might, for there is no work, nor device, nor knowledge, nor wisdom, in the grave, whither thou goest."

Such a gloomy text, Vecto thought, fitting for Gyro. It was his favorite for some reason. He leaned over and a device that was stuck behind his orb exited his shield. He clutched it firmly and ejected a blade. "I believe this is yours," Vecto said aloud as he looked at the cross in his hand. He retrieved it this morning, just for Gyro. He let it filter through his hand and stabbed it into the grave.

Slowly, he rose.

"If I were a human, I would hate myself," he said as if Gyro could hear.

"And why's that?" Gyro would have asked.

"I would have … tears," Vecto said, as if replying. "Farewell, my friend," he said as he walked away, pacing down the hill as wind swirled a dust cloud by. It blanketed the hilltop, fading Gyro's gravesite within the sky.

Vecto descended the steep hill, glancing at the trees he passed by. It was a miracle they survived, he thought. He noticed one tree that split its branches within the ground, then came up only to merge overhead, forming a dome of protection for planetary creatures. Then another tree grew horizontally, slithering over the ground with its branches planted heavily in the surface. Such weird plants, he thought, adaptive plants created by men to help excrete oxygen in the air. There were supposed to be many, to ease the conversion power of atmospheric generators, but not on this war planet.

"So he's finally coming down the hill," Accura said, lying flat on a cliff with her sniper rifle set up on a stand. She was nearly six miles away, waiting for Vecto's descent. "You're my bounty, Vecto, no one else's." Her mechanical eye zoomed in to see Vecto casually walking down the slope. He had that red suit image activated—the same as the first time they met—but this time, according to X-ray, he was weaponless.

"Just a little farther," she said to herself, wanting him to walk on the straight path, away from the dust clouds. "You can't sense me now," she said, knowing his Lapton map only had a radius of 5.25 miles.

"I've got you now," Accura said, steadying her sniper

rifle. She had it pointed at his orb. Four bullets would fire in rapid succession. The first would splatter on his outer shield, creating a portal for the next three to pass through. The second and third bullets would take care of Vecto's other two shields and the final one would strike the orb, blowing it up. Such inventive shells, although expensive. Her tactic should do the trick.

"Lower my pulse," she said to her computer. Her armor injected a substance through her veins to decrease her heart rate and slow her blood. Although the bullets were propelled by a force of opposing molecules rather than explosions—thereby making the shots silent, steady and deadly—the distance made it troublesome. She only had one shot at this, so she had to make it count.

Life is such a strange concept, Vecto mused as his feet stepped on black, hardened mud that collapsed into goop. *Perhaps I've misjudged myself. Perhaps Leroy Johnson was correct in his assessment—that I have emotions after all. If only I had a soul, as humans call it, then conceivably, I could understand its full extent. If only—*

Four silent bullets slipped through the air, struck Vecto's shields in succession. Then there was an explosion and he disappeared from sight.

"Mission accomplished," Accura said with a smirk, proud of her excellent shot. She had it aimed at his orb, and there was no way Vecto was fast enough to dodge them. All she had to do now was collect his orb's remains to collect her bounty. To be certain of his destruction, she zoomed in on his remains. Only—Vecto was standing there, looking directly at her.

"Blast it! How did he live?" She quickly sniped more

bullets his way. But Vecto burst mud into the air, causing the bullet portals to stick to muck rather than his shields. They acted as an extra barrier for the bullets to pass through, causing the fourth bullet in the series to explode prematurely.

"I don't have time for you," Vecto said, knowing she couldn't hear him. He was rotating a barrier of black mud over him, sucking carbon from underneath him. It was by fortune that Vecto had some mud inside his shields as a carbon source when Accura fired her first rounds. Otherwise, he would have indeed been destroyed.

He zoomed in on Accura on the cliff in the distance, rotating the mud around him even faster as bullets splattered and blew up around him. When she ran out of ammo, Vecto launched the mud at her.

Accura quickly formed a shield over her arm as thousands of hardened mud particles splattered against it. The mud was slung at bullet speeds, rapidly slaughtering her sniper rifle at her side and pounding the cliff. She watched the mud bullets tatter the sniper gun to pieces. Then the mudslinging stopped.

Accura breathed heavily, despite the sedative still in her blood stream. The cliff could have been severely unstable. She had to be careful when sliding back from the cliff, as not to disturb the weakened structure. Slowly, she crawled backward, but she felt a foot strike her in the spine.

"Going somewhere?" Feit asked.

"Who are you?" Accura snapped back.

"I'd like to ask you the same thing."

While facedown, Accura quickly grabbed her handgun to her side and blindly shot in his direction.

Feit leaned back as the bullet grazed his face. It gave Accura time to roll away.

She spun to her feet and fired again, but Feit had kicked up a piece of the destroyed sniper rifle, grabbed it, and used it as a shield. Accura pointed the gun at him point blank.

"Drop the weapon!" she yelled.

Feit let the piece drop. "Why were you targeting that man?"

"That being is no man," Accura stated. "It's a machine wanted by Acaterran government, and it is my duty to destroy it."

"Well it's my job to watch it," Feit responded. He quickly grabbed the nozzle of her gun and detached it from the handle, disassembling the gun in front of her eyes. "You're coming with me," he said, spinning the gun nozzle in his hand.

But the sting of a sword's edge pressed against Feit's back. "Leave her alone," another voice demanded.

Feit turned his head see a boy from the corner of his eye. "And you are?"

"Chais!?" Accura exclaimed. "What are you doing on this planet? Wait, have you been—have you been following me?" she asked annoyed.

"Hello to you, too," Chais said sarcastically then looked at Feit. "Now drop whatever that is in your hand!"

"It would be in your best interest, sir, if you, too, dropped that sword," Feit said.

"Or what?" Chais asked with a smirk.

Feit dropped the nozzle and suddenly leaned forward. He did a back kick to knock the hilt of Chais' blade as he snatched the falling nozzle. He then completed the full turn of the kick and drove the gun nozzle up to block Chais' swing. The sword and nozzle clashed, but Chais flipped a switch and the blade divided into two, forming an "X." Chais quickly twisted his wrist, thrusting the sword from its side blade. The blade scraped Feit's tunic as he dodged.

"Both of you, freeze!" Accura yelled with yet another gun in her hand.

Feit and Chais stopped in their tracks.

She looked down at the cliff, which was starting to crack.

"Now listen up!" Accura ordered. "This cliff is already unstable, so unless you two want to plummet nearly a mile down, I'd suggest we all get off this ledge!"

Feit and Chais looked down to see the crack growing. Feit did a backward flip out of the way as Chais shrugged and walked behind it.

"You, too, Accura," Chais said, nonchalantly waving his hand. But as Accura took light steps, the crack suddenly burst across. She looked up at Chais as the edge of the cliff crumbled and broke off, taking her with it.

"Noo!!" Chais yelled, reaching his hand out to catch her. But she was too far to catch.

Feit looked over the new edge. "I'm sorry," he said, shaking his head.

Chais ignored him and leaped off the cliff after her.

"Accura!" he yelled as he burst through a dust cloud after her. He could see her now. She was fiddling with her militaristic outfit. There was no way he could reach her going at the same speed.

She then activated her parachute.

Chais was stunned as the chute unraveled before him. With a jolt, Accura's speed had stopped but Chais was headed for a collision course. He smacked into the parachute, and his sword dug into it to break his fall.

"You idiot!" Accura yelled, realizing Chais had jumped

after her and destroyed her parachute.

He got tangled in the cords and bumped into her. "Don't worry about it—I gotcha!" Chais yelled.

"More like killing me!" Accura yelled back.

Chais wasn't concerned. He detached his blade from its handle and let it dangle loose from the chain holding them together. He then twirled the blade in the air by the chain and propelled it at the cliff. The sword stabbed into the rock as rough hooks on the sides of the blade held it in place. But as the slack wore off, Chais and Accura jolted and swung toward the precipice. Accura had to throw a Forb at the cliff to ease the collision. The orb struck the cliff and released purple foam to act as a cushion. Chais slammed into it while holding Accura in his arms as Accura's torn parachute glided over them.

"Not bad!" Chais said, laughing, shoving the parachute off him.

Accura looked down at the fall. "And how do you suppose we get back up?" she questioned.

"Don't worry, babe," Chais said as he clicked his handle to real them in. "I've got ya."

The two were lifted to the sword as Accura ejected her tangled parachute. Now they had to climb the rest of the way up.

It took quite a while to scale the cliff, but Chais and Accura met the challenge.

Sitting cross-legged at the top of the cliff was Feit. Behind him were sparse trees decorating a hill, with a military rail station in the distant background. He sat quietly, watching as Chais' gloved hand snatched the top of the cliff.

With a yank, Chais slung Accura to the top, and she lifted herself the rest of the way. She reached down to grab

Chais' hand to help him up. Chais struggled to get his weary feet on the surface, then rolled to his back, out of breath.

"Seems like you need more exercise," Feit said, his eyes fixed on them.

Chais and Accura were startled.

"What? Did ya wait here just to kill us?" Chais yelled, attempting to stand, reaching for his sword.

"There's no need for that," Feit responded, standing up with his arms crossed. "You two are clearly not fit for battle."

"Then what do you want?" Accura yelled.

"It's not what I want," Feit answered, shifting his eyes to look beyond them.

Chais and Accura looked back to see what it was. Floating in front of the cliff was a red-suited figure with the face of Robert Newman.

"You!" Chais yelled. "You're the one who turned me in and stole my diamond cross!"

"Vecto!" Accura exclaimed.

Chais' eyes bulged. "Vecto? Did you say Vecto?!"

"I see I have quite the following," Vecto stated as he hovered to the cliff.

Chais readied his sword and Accura raised her gun as they both stepped back from the approaching machine.

Vecto lightly landed before them, gazing at the three fighters. "There's no need for weaponry. I am not here for a fight."

"You killed a hundred or so innocent soldiers!" Accura yelled. "How are you not here to kill us?"

"I regret my previous actions while in rage," Vecto explained. "I have no intention of furthering any strife."

"You've already done the damage, bub," Chais said,

looking away.

"You must understand," Vecto said. "My focus is on Morphaal alone. This I have realized. You trio are not my enemies."

"Oh, so I get it," Chais laughed, rubbing his face. "Now you want to apologize, huh?"

Vecto paused. "What I seek is your support."

Chais and Accura, even Feit, were set aback by Vecto's response.

"I am a member of the Alpha Squad," Vecto explained. "Without a team, we are ineffective. Only with teamwork have we beaten Morphaal before. I was erroneous to believe I could kill him on my own."

"Whoa, whoa," Chais stumbled on his words, still shocked. "You mean you want us to join the Alpha Squad after trying to kill us?"

Feit walked between Accura and Chais. "What's the condition? Slavery?"

Vecto shook his head. "I merely seek assistance in my quest to defeat Morphaal. All three of you are capable fighters. So what will it be?"

"No," Accura was the first to deny his offer. "You killed innocent lives and have a steep bounty on your head—your orb, whatever. I cannot and will not associate with you!"

"Bounty?" Chais said, curious as to how much. He scratched his chin. "Well I dunno. What's in it for me?"

"Saving the omniverse," Vecto replied.

Chais thought about it.

But Feit shook his head. "Not likely. My duty lies with Master Johnson. My task is to keep you under watch."

"Then logically, you must come with me," Vecto told Feit. "And you, Accura, will likely follow in your attempt to assassinate me." He looked at Chais. "And Chais, the bounty on Morphaal's head is far greater than on mine."

Chais smirked as the others fell silent.

"So, inevitably, if you want to join me or not, all three of you will still be following me to Morphaal," Vecto reasoned. "And if you want to or not, you will be forced in battle with him. If it takes you to be my enemies to be my allies in battle, then so be it."

The face of Robert Newman smirked as he strolled by them to leave.

Feit, Chais, and Accura looked at each other, bewildered, knowing he had a point.

"So then where are you going next? What if I tell the officials on the ship who you are?" Accura asked, pushing Chais out of the way.

"I'm not going back to the ship," Vecto said as he walked off. "Follow me if you wish, but you wouldn't tell them. It'll widen your competition in claiming any bounty."

Chais rushed over to Vecto. "So how much are we talk'n about—for killing Morphaal?"

"Enough to buy your own planet," Vecto stated.

Chais' grinned at the thought of so much money.

"Vecto, you fool!" Feit yelled. "Even if all four of us fought Morphaal, we wouldn't stand a chance. I have heard horror stories about that brute sadist defeating legions of men."

Vecto stopped, then looked back as a nearby tree bristled in the wind. "It only took four A.S. members to defeat him before," he replied.

"So how are we supposed to follow that jerk if he just flies off?" Chais asked, stepping over a ground tree.

"Azmeck will likely know his destination," Feit calmly stated, walking through the small forest with his hands cupped behind his back.

"He'll be on Cubix," Accura said, while staying her distance from Feit.

"What are you, psychic?" Chais wondered.

"You two said it yourselves—he's looking for a planet called Zendora to find Morphaal. Then he's likely to visit his homeworld to ask the Dinishmen if they know where it is, seeing they're the smartest beings in existence."

"And how's he supposed to get there without getting back on the ship?" Chais questioned. "Fly there?"

Accura shook her head and brushed her long, black hair behind her ear. "Hodos has teleportation stations."

"What's that?" Chais asked.

"You know, instant travel?" Accura answered, curious as to whether he was serious. His look suggested he was. "Oh brother," she said with a sigh. "The Dinishmen helped the Magnatronians with technical advancements during the Magus war, and they set up instant teleportation from Hodos to Cubix."

"Oh, I see," Chais said, resting his sword against his shoulder. "So we hitch a ride with the rail system like we did before but this time to this teleportation place."

"Except I'm going alone," Accura stated, brushing leaves out of the way to see the massive rail-transportation facility ahead. "And don't follow me."

"Hey, I was following this guy," Chais defended himself, pointing at Feit. "Who, uh, happened to be following you."

"My name's Feit," Feit said, tired of being called "this guy" and "that guy."

"Fate?" Chais said with a laugh. "Didn't know an ape

can determine the future."

Feit stopped in his tracks and reached his hand out to stop Chais behind him. "From here on, you're going to shut your mouth. We're in Magnatronian territory, and if they see us or hear us, they won't hesitate to throw us in jail."

"Nothing new to me," Chais said matter-of-factly. "Just came from one."

Accura leaned her foot against a ground tree truck and zoomed in on the mechanical facility with her eye. She saw bulky militia transports drive up a ramp, then attach to the magnetic rail above and hook in place. When the transports were all interlocked together, they sped off in a group in a monorail-like train. It was designed to consume little to no energy, as the magnetic rail propelled the carriers forward. It was also the heaviest-guarded area. Plenty of soldiers roamed the grounds, safeguarding their military supplies. She would have to sneak onboard a transport before it latched to the rail.

"Not many open spots like before," Chais whispered. "Any ideas?" he asked Accura, then looked behind him.

She was missing. He glanced around and saw her heading west. They were facing northwest.

"There she goes, again," Chais mumbled to himself. "Hey Feit, we'll—"

Feit was gone also, headed straight.

"Well, jeez. Leave me behind, will ya!" Chais pointed his sword in each of their direction as if a compass. "I guess that means I go this way." He twirled the blade in his hand as he walked northbound.

It wasn't long before the Magnatronians spotted Accura. She kept her distance, but when the planetary warriors saw her and closed in, she could only surrender.

Fighting these soldiers-by-birth with little weaponry was unwise. The same held true for Feit, who eliminated one Magnatronian only to be surrounded by many.

But Chais, on the other hand, was boldly standing on the rail with his sword over his shoulder and his trench coat snapping in the wind. He cocked his head back, staring at the two suns in the sky, waiting for the next train to slip by. He could feel vibrations as the magnetic pulse from the rail activated, propelling the transport train forward. It was faster than Chais expected, so he took a leap of faith off the rail, timing his fall.

The train passed underneath as Chais landed hard on its roof. He tumbled across the rough surface, rolling from crate to crate as he tried to use his sword to stop his inertia. No good. The train took a sharp turn, tilting on its side as Chais slipped off the roof. But when the transport tilted back in place, Chais was hanging from its side. His gloved hand adhered to the surface as his other hand grasped his sword. His body swung as he looked down at how far up he actually was.

I knew I shouldn't have looked down, Chais scolded himself as he got sick. Sure, climbing up to the rail was no problem, but realizing how far up he truly was, that was a bit unsettling. Not wanting to stay hanging around, Chais used his upper-arm strength to lift himself to a window. He retracted his sword to its smaller size and sheathed it in his wildly blowing cloak, freeing his other hand. Only problem was a Magnatronian stared at him from the transport's window as Chais climbed over it.

"Uh, just thought I'd stick around," Chais said with a weak smile, waiving. All he could see now was a fist coming at him. He quickly rolled to the side as the Magnatronian punched through the window and grabbed

Chais' foot. Chais squirmed his foot free—out of its boot—as the Magnatronian crushed the footwear in his grasp and stuck his head out from the shattered glass.

Chais scaled the train to its roof and rolled to his back hoping the Magnatronian wasn't stupid enough to come after him. Yet, Chais was curious. He rolled and looked over the edge despite his somewhat fear of heights. Unbelievably, the Magnatronian had stepped out from the window, completely vertical. He was walking on the side of the transport as if it was the ground.

Chais rolled back over, not believing his eyes. He quickly unsheathed his sword and extended the blade.

With his Magnatronian battle armor, the soldier had his center of gravity adjusted and his feet adherent so he could walk vertically.

Chais watched as the Magnatronian's foot stepped on the edge. He took a step in the air and his body suddenly leaned up. With ease, his suit adjusted to the changed axis—the soldier was slung upright, slamming his foot on the roof as his head rose menacingly.

"Uh, hi there," Chais said as his no-longer-slicked-back brown hair jetted to the side. "I take it you like the breeze, too."

"Get off this train," the Magnatronian ordered.

Chais looked up as the single white poles that held up the rail blurred by. "Guess I'll have to wait till the next stop," Chais joked as he looked back at the soldier with his sword ready. "Not supposed to exit a moving train."

The Magnatronian shook his head. He clutched his fist and nanobites from his suit began to retract. The small, microscopic machines crawled up his arms in retreat and slithered from his face to show his dull expression. They then traveled down his chest to reveal his muscle shirt underneath, and settled in a compartment behind his back, leaving only his waist and legs covered by the suit.

"I'll throw you off," the Magnatronian said as his chest muscles flexed.

"Some strict zero tolerance policy you've got there," Chais cut back, slashing his sword to his side. "Well, I won't let you!" He quickly came at the Magnatronian, swinging his sword at him with swift speed, despite missing a shoe.

It was blocked by a knife. The Magnatronian stood there with his hand raised, blocking the pressing sword with his knife held upside down.

It was time for Chais' little trick. He hit a switch and another blade snapped into place to form an elongated Phillips head. With a thrust and twist of the wrist, Chais lunged the side blade at the soldier's chest. The warrior neither dodged nor blocked the sword. He let it stab into his shoulder.

Green blood seeped from his body as Chais looked up at the beast, his sword still within his chest.

The Magnatronian smirked, then grabbed the blade with his hand and pulled it from his body. Chais was overpowered as the man moved his sword to the side and punched him in the gut with brute force.

The next thing Chais knew, he was tumbling on the roof and was once again hanging from the side as the transport banked around another turn.

"Great! A super-warrior," Chais muttered as he lifted himself up.

The Magnatronian was right there, staring at him. He reached down and grabbed Chais by the throat, lifting him up to his level. Chais' feet dangled in the air off the edge of the train. He gasped as he struggled to free his throat from the impending contusion and suffocation. He grabbed a pouch from his cloak and smashed it into the Magnatronian's face. A powdery substance puffed in the soldier's eyes as Chais squinted. The soldier growled, unable to see, but didn't let go. He threw Chais off the train instead.

Chais quickly swung his sword and detached the blade as he flew off. The blade smashed through a window and snagged something. Chais held tight as he was swung to the train traveling hundreds of miles per hour. He smashed into another window several crates back and rolled into boxes of weaponry.

Five Magnatronians stood there, guarding the inventory.

"OK, OK, I give up!" Chais reluctantly said as he lifted pain-stricken arms.

"Ah, Vecto," Admiral Keefe said as Vecto approached him in the barely lit hanger bay of military base Bloodstain. He was inspecting rows of air-to-space aircraft fighters, looking for incisions made from battle.

"Sir, requesting permission to teleport to Cubix," Vecto asked, standing upright.

"Don't have to ask, son," Keefe answered. "You know the answer. Wanna take the doc with ya?" Keefe looked over as if to point out where Dr. Azmeck was standing. "These men don't like Terrans roamin' around."

Azmeck noticed Vecto from across the room and began walking toward them.

"I'll take him back to the ship," Vecto replied.

"Oh, and by the way," Keefe said as he trailed his fingers across a jet, "some guards near the Unilift rail facility captured some Terrans sneaking around. Three I believe, not far from Gyro's gravesite. Are they with you?"

"No."

"Good. The soldiers were want'n to have some live, hand-to-hand combat."

"Take them to the Corona when you're done," Vecto stated.

Keefe smirked. "All right, only 'cause you helped us in the war," he said. "Been a pleasure. Tell the Dinishmen at the teleport station I sent you."

Vecto nodded as Keefe carried on with his inspection and as Azmeck approached.

"Quite discourteous of you to leave me behind like that!" Azmeck stated, holding his back.

"You're going back to the ship," Vecto said, ignoring Azmeck's comment.

"Then where might you be going, eh?" Azmeck asked.

"I'm going to talk with Vic to see if he knows anything about Zendora."

"Ah, then perhaps I should mention the robots on the Corona."

"You're not going."

"It is pertinent that I speak with him also."

"Why?"

"Because those machines are of his making, and I'm afraid they were sold to a renegade bounty hunter."

"Who?" Vecto questioned.

Azmeck sighed. "A bounty hunter with devastating intentions, that's who."

07

Vecto decided to still leave without Azmeck. He glanced at the Dinishman working the controls of his teleportation booth. The pale, bald midget smirked. Although Vecto was under disguise, the being from his homeworld knew who he was. Vecto was scanned as part of the teleportation process, but the Hodos-based Dinishmen wouldn't turn him into Acaterran police—Vecto was sure—the Magnatronians wouldn't have it.

In a fast, high-pitched dialect, the Dinishman finally spoke. "We welcome you to our teleportation station and wish you safe travels to planet Cubix in the Parallel Universe Geom where you will be transferred to point 25261316 in Sector 5 Vecto, although we sincerely advise you not to visit our world in light of your dire standing with the Ukase Order."

"I am quite capable of handling myself," Vecto stated.

The Dinishman worked for the Magnatronians rather than Cubix' governing body, referred to as Ukase. If anything, the little guy was more worried about him being caught by the Ukase than the Acaterran government.

The Dinishman nodded and flipped a switch.

Vecto stood at the center of a round platform. Hovering over his head was a white disk. Lasers shot down from sixteen sides of the disk to form a cylindrical circumference around him. It was followed by the formation of a shield. Vecto looked up as the disk opened to reveal the sky of Cubix. The round platform below him then moved, pushing him toward the sky. Vecto's body was slowly lifted through the portal. He rose up from the surface of Cubix, being transferred to the streets rather than inside the nearby teleportation facility. It looked like his human body image was cut in half as he was lifted the rest of the way. When the lift stopped, Vecto stepped off of it and the portal disappeared.

It had been a while since he stepped foot on his homeworld. Not only was he disowned from his creator, he was despised by the Ukase due to his rebellion of the system.

Vecto scanned his surroundings to update his Lapton map. He watched as Dinishmen filled the streets, chatting to themselves. They were communicating to others far off through invisible teleportation of sound waves. The high-pitched sound they spoke would instantly be transmitted to another Dinishman's brain. They spoke so quickly in their Dinix tongue that their voices sounded like brief whistles.

Others walked by but disappeared in mid-stride. They were being teleported to other areas of the planet.

There were no product advertisements on this planet, unlike the numerous billboard Nexus screens that bombarded metropolitan cities on Acaterra. It was a relief to Vecto, who preferred simplicity. Acaterra's economy had a consumption tax system, which translated into lots of thought-recognition advertisements by the government that targeted ads based on surrounding thought waves. Cubix, however, was an idea-driven society controlled by the Ukase.

Although Acaterra was mostly governmental owned as well, Cubix was unique in that it had no currency. Dinishmen were provided with a social rank and living amenities based on their scientific contributions. Their governing system allowed Dinishmen to remain the most advanced race in the omniverse, and with no currency, it kept their world self-sustaining without outside planetary trade except through the governing body.

Vecto saw the Ukase bank ahead, the only bank on the planet; it was the one where he caught a human swindle drifter upon his creation twenty-one years ago. He recalled it was his first good deed, yet one that ironically led to his discovering. No one knew the government was spying on them—not until it was revealed later.

Vecto strolled across the white surface. He had to keep his disguise. The ground was watching him, listening—so were the walls, the structures, everything around him. It absorbed colors, thus recorded images. The entire city consisted of this white augmentation substance referred to as Augere Crescere. It could grow into buildings, restructure on its own, and maintain a polished, dirt-free appearance. The planet had no star except a white dwarf, yet Cubix' bright core emitted light through its crystalloid surface, which was then absorbed by the city's ground and transmitted throughout. The city glowed but appeared not to. Shadows were sparse in the metropolis.

"Hey you!" a human shouted to a Dinishman far off while brandishing a gun.

Vecto picked up on the distant conversation.

"Come on now, give me all your money," the man ordered.

Stupid human, Vecto thought.

The Ukase knew he was there, as the spyware flagged his weapon. The Dinishman disappeared, automatically being transported to safety. To the man's surprise, the ground enveloped his feet to restrain him. The thwarted thief bewilderedly fired at the surface, but he disappeared as well, teleported to confinement. The crescere returned to normal, repairing itself and disintegrating contaminants.

It was that easy to have justice, Vecto thought, but that much easier to take freedom away.

Hours passed and Vecto was at the outskirts of the city. Shadows were in abundance now, as there was no ground except the crystallic surface. Light shone from the planet's core, creating a long shadow above Vecto as he approached Vic's lab. He mused at how Vic would react to his return.

He walked by crystallic carbon ice pillars that melted upon his presence and came to the enormous silver door of Vic's facility. The holographic image of a robot's head formed in front of the massive, silver door, followed by a mechanical voice.

"Identify yourself," it commanded.

"Vecto Botland," Vecto simply replied.

The image flickered and yet another holograph popped out. It was an eye, which upon release scanned Vecto.

"You're appearance is that of a human, but our scans indicate otherwise," the voice said.

Vecto dropped his image to reveal his orb surrounded by mud.

The robot continued. "Match approved. We have

anticipated your arrival."

Vecto found his statement unsettling. He waited, but the door didn't budge. Instead, the soft, whistle sound of teleportation surrounded him. Dozens of robots were teleported outside, and they weren't the welcoming committee.

"It would be unwise if you seek to battle," Vecto stated, hovering his orb to the center as robots shuffled around. He created another false image, this time a replica of the bulky, one-piece body Gyro created for him. "I'd suggest you let me in. Otherwise, Vic would have plenty of recyclable materials."

The lead robot, identified by a red stripe across its black body, stepped out from the crowd. "You are classified as dangerous by the Acaterran government and, therefore, we must take necessary precautions."

Vecto would have laughed. These weren't even the Botland series robots. They were Peril series fighters. Even with one hundred eighteen of them surrounding him, Vecto saw no immediate threat.

"Take your best shot," Vecto teased.

The lead bot formed a ball of energy in his gun as he zipped by. His hand emerged from the large cylinder gun nozzle, grasping the energy and slamming it into Vecto's shielded head. Vecto simply grabbed its arm, twisted it until metal shards spattered in the air, then yanked it, letting the robot's body fly by and dig into the crystallic surface. The other robots remained still, with guns pointed at him as Vecto reached down to grab the remains of their leader. He lifted the limp body in front of him and kept it there as its head slowly melted from Vecto's shields.

In a wave of firepower, the other machines retaliated. Zero point energy blasts bombarded Vecto's shields from all sides. Vecto was calm, standing in the center of the light show, until finally his image disappeared and his shields expanded like an explosion. Robots were struck by the outer shield, crushed and blasted away from the force of the expansion. When the explosion stopped, other robots shattered; with no visible explanation, their heads caved in, their bodies lifted in the air and flew into pillars of carbon ice. They were being grabbed by invisible arms of the shield, tossed, crushed, shattered, slung into each other—Vecto's Flummox Capacitor orb hovered in the middle as the robots were destroyed in mere seconds.

Missiles came at Vecto and struck his shields, and Vecto at last retracted his FFS, reforming his robotic image. Arms, legs, torsos, and heads showered as the remaining robots readied their guns.

Vecto dropped his image, his orb hovered in the air. Slowly, pieces of scrap metal quivered or rolled. They abruptly zipped in the air, clanging to his orb through magnetic force. The pieces formed around Vecto, shaping a physical body for him. His face formed out of tiny pieces of metal, and his arm consisted of thousands of parts held together by his Force Field Shields.

"Come at me," Vecto taunted, motioning with his newly-created hand.

The robots inched forward.

What appeared to be wires blasted from around Vecto's robotic body. They latched onto the machines, pulling them, tossing them, severing them. They grabbed the last two and yanked them in as Vecto grabbed their heads and smashed them into the crystallic ice below.

All robots were accounted for. All were gone. Slowly, Vecto stood.

"D.E.-termination program activated," a robotic voice

said from behind.

Vecto turned around to see three silver Botland series robots blocking the entrance to Vic's lab.

"It is about time you showed up," Vecto stated. He rushed the center bot and clasped hands with it. It already had its "mock" Force Field Shields activated. Mock shields, that's what Vecto called them.

The robot slid back but held its ground.

"Only I have the true FFS," Vecto stated, pressing his power against his. "Yours is only a MIMIC!"

Vecto overpowered its shield and thrust his right arm. The robot's arm crushed from the sheer force—its joint buckled and split as if a shattered log of wood. Its other arm was pulled by Vecto at the same time—its elbow ripped apart, shattering pieces in the air. Vecto lifted the machine by the slit forehead and stabbed the ripped-off arm in its chest.

Another Botland robot fired a charged O.E blast at Vecto. It impacted his robotic image and pushed him back. Vecto discarded the motionless robot in his grasp and lunged his arm at the other, extending it to reach the machine, but the Botland robot leaped out of the way and fired again. It was accompanied by the third machine. Vecto rushed at the later one and pounded its chest. The robot smashed through a pillar but quickly emerged from the falling shattered ice—shadows rising from each piece. The robot transported a fist over its mounted gun-arm, grabbed a falling shard of the carbon ice and zipped to Vecto. It stabbed Vecto's shield with it and rapidly pounded its fists into Vecto's chest as pieces scattered in the air.

Vecto slid back as the rapid force ensued, but he formed his outer shield over the robot's arms, destabilized its shield and severed its limbs. The machine executed a head butt, but Vecto came full force with his. Their heads collided, metal shattered, and Vecto emerged as the one with the hardest head.

Vecto looked back at the last Botland series machine.

"I apologize for our behavior, prototype Vecto," the robot said, kneeling. "We must follow our master's orders."

Vecto walked up to the lead bot. He needed his cooperation. Not even Vecto could bust into Vic's lab by force—not when it was covered in valignium, the strongest metal known in existence.

He suddenly dropped his outer shield, and his pieced-together body dismantled, collapsing to the ground.

"Then I will be your new master," Vecto said.

Moments later, Vecto was walking down curved, dark hallways. His orb nestled neatly inside the Botland series robot's hollow chest. It was a bit odd controlling his new body, better than being inside Azmeck's robot, however. At least he had access to the building.

The interior of the barely lit building was rigid, with rows of robots behind glass walls as showcases. Vecto ignored the machines and came to a five-foot-tall door with the words, "Vic's Lab Room," both in English and Dinix.

Before he could knock, or break the door in, his bald-headed midget creator, Vic, opened the door.

"I see you are quite the persistent and stubborn one in soliciting my advice my derelict robot creation Vecto," Vic's high-pitched voice hastily said. "However I do not know the whereabouts of Zendora only that it is located in the innerverse and believed to be surrounded by black holes to prohibit its location from being discovered."

"I presume Azmeck called," Vecto said.

Vic laughed and looked down. A seat lifted from a portal in the ground, bringing Vic's three-foot-tall body to eye level. "As should you have because it would have saved you the trip but I was hoping you'd say I was psychic."

Vecto shook his head. "I apologize for wasting my time with you, Master Vic," Vecto stated as he turned to leave. "If you are unaware of how to get to Zendora, then I have no purpose in staying."

Vic honked his liftseat's horn to get Vecto's attention. "Alas there may be a way to find its location with my latest super-intellectual creation the Illuminous Orb."

Vecto stopped to glance back at Vic. It wouldn't hurt to ask his so called "super-intelligent" creation. "Lead the way," he demanded.

Vic led Vecto to a door boarded by valignium. Only through Vic's authority and coordinates could they teleport within. Inside were brilliant lights filling the massive globe. They rode a platform to the center of the spherical room. Hovering in the center were over fifty orbs layered together and working in tandem to produce intelligence far beyond any known system.

Vic smirked as he gazed up at his creation. "Imagine the unfathomable power of your Flummox Capacitor in that. If one can produce artificial intelligence at that caliber, what can a replica of multiple AIs within a cascaded system of Force Field Shield orbs accomplish?"

Vecto glanced down at Vic. "I get the idea. So how does it work?"

"You must place your hand on it and it will speak," Vic directed. "Huuk guas he uoot ehtue ua ak jeuou. ... don't you hear it? They sing to each other in my voice," Vic translated his Dinix phrase though it was unnecessary.

Vecto couldn't pick up any odd sound waves. He shook his head and complied, flexing the mechanical fingers of his hand and reaching out to the compilation of moving orbs. He touched it, but briefly. His shields flickered from the massive energy excreted from them.

"Where … is … planet Zendora?" Vecto asked the machine.

The orbs glowed momentarily but did nothing more.

He touched it again, more firmly. "Where is Zendora?" he yelled.

The orbs glowed more excessively, as if they were going to explode, then the light shut off and the orbs rotated to a stop.

Vecto stood back. "It appears your machine is broken," Vecto stated.

"Eeee!" Vic screeched, looking over the massive orb, quite worried. Yet the orbs suddenly came back to life, resuming their individual movements around each other. Vic smiled, but not for long. "You imbecile. You have done quite enough damage already to my robots first and now this."

"Your machines attacked me first," Vecto retaliated. "It would not have been a problem if you had just let me in."

"You know I can't do that with Ukase's tight leash on society and my reputation at stake."

"Self-centered as always, Master Vic," Vecto said.

Vic grumble under his breath and moved the hovering platform from the core.

Vecto looked back at the orb. Useless junk, he thought. He figured it wasn't going to work. If he and AI Sarah didn't know where Zendora was, why would this machine?

He looked back at Vic. "There's one more thing I need to know."

Vic glanced up at him a bit irritated. "What is it now?"

"Dr. Azmeck observed that the Corona exploration ship has robots aboard that you created and sold to a bounty hunter. My data log identifies them as Viper classification."

Vic thought about it. "They must be the machines I manufactured for the Ukase a few months back but why were they there? They are designed for military purposes only and not for a civilian ship."

"Perhaps they are being transported," Vecto reasoned. "Perhaps this guy is waiting for his pick-up."

"Then you mustn't let him retrieve the machines if he intends to use them for destructive purposes!"

"And why do you care?" Vecto said. "You never did about me."

Vic screeched the platform to a halt at the wall of the globe. "It's not if I care Vecto, it's if you do that truly matters."

Incidentally, as Vecto headed back to Sector 5's teleportation center to leave Cubix, he saw Chais shivering outside, trying to bum money from a Dinishman.

Vecto shook his head at the sight, knowing Chais wouldn't get anywhere panhandling. Dinishmen don't own cash—thanks to Cubix's currency-less system.

One of his initial reactions seeing Chais, however, was why Chais was even on this planet. He would have had to get approval on planet Hodos first. *Either he convinced the Magnatronians in an attempt to follow me or they banished him here so they wouldn't have to deal with him.* He picked both.

"I see you're following me," Vecto said.

Chais spun around in alarm and scratched his head as the Dinishman he was talking to teleported himself away. "Hey, gotta follow the money, you know. So about that bounty?" Chais asked, casually strolling to Vecto as he slipped an item in his pocket.

Vecto did a quick analysis and realized that Chais pickpocketed the Dinishman. Amazingly, he did it without the Ukase knowing through the all-seeing Crescere substance surrounding him. Vecto decided not to bring attention to the matter. If he said anything, the Ukase would interfere and Vecto would be questioned, in effect blowing his cover.

"What bounty?" Vecto responded.

"The guy you're after—Morphaal."

"What about it?"

"I'm a pretty strong guy. You're going to need some help fighting him, remember?" Chais said, closing his trench coat for warmth. "I decided I'll tag along and collect my share of bounty when the job's done."

"In the condition you stay out of my way," Vecto said, motioning him to follow as he walked into the teleportation building.

Chais took that as yes. "Then it's a deal. Any more leads?"

"Unfortunately not."

"So where to next?"

"Back to the ship."

Chais slowed his pace and squinted. "Wait a sec. That's a no-zone for me. They'll put me back into jail, man."

"That's the point."

"Ha, ha, funny," Chais said. He had a better idea for their new destination, somewhere he'd been yearning to go since Vecto first told him about the world. "How 'bout

Earth? We can go there. What do you say?"

"It's not a vacation. And there's not much worth seeing," Vecto said as they got in line. He recalled that when he first met Chais, the kid inquired a lot about Earth, and how it favored Zendora to some extent—before Earth went to waste. Perhaps he thought it would be the closest he'll get to his homeworld since the chances of them finding it were growing slimmer..

"Ah, loosen up," Chais said. "We can find some clues."

"Hardly. There's nothing there but ruins, rocks, and the Nagora clan—not to mention the gravity."

Chais did a double take. "Huh, what'd ya say?"

"The gravity—it's intense."

"Nah, not that—the clan. What's it called?"

"Nagora."

Chais stroked his chin. "Hey, you know, come to think of it, I think I've heard that name before."

"I've mentioned it to you when we first met."

"No, like I've heard it on Zendora."

It caught Vecto's attention. He paused to hear his answer.

Chais mulled the thought in his head for a few seconds and remembered where he heard it. "Yeah, from history class. My tutor said something about a clan of alien ninjas who crashed on our planet. I'd swear she said they were called the Nagora clan."

"And you didn't tell me this beforehand?"

"Huh? What's the big deal? Didn't think about it till now," Chais said, rubbing his arms for warmth. It was cold even inside the building.

If the Nagora clan had visited Zendora in the past, perhaps they have a record of it and know where the planet is, Vecto thought. He could ask his old friend Shadow.

"Well, if you're not going, I'm going alone," Chais said. "Maybe they can lead me to Morphaal and I can get the bounty for myself."

"You'll die fighting him alone," Vecto stated. "Upon analysis, I've decided to go to old Earth after all."

Chais smirked but wondered about the Corona. "What about the ship? Wouldn't you miss the ride?"

"The repairs on Corona are not scheduled to be completed for a week," Vecto responded. He figured he could worry about the robots on the ship later. They wouldn't be a threat until they were delivered anyway, he figured. It was more important to find Morphaal.

"All right, then, Earth it is," Chais said, stretching his arms.

08

The two were transported to old Earth downward instead of up. The gravity was too intense for an upward transport so they went feet first for their safety.

As Chais descended into the transport disk, it felt like his feet were being yanked from the other side. When his whole body exited the transport, he crashed to his knees and fell face-first into the dirt. Vecto landed effortlessly beside him.

Vecto wasn't kidding about the gravity, Chais thought. It must have been ten times what he was used to. It forced him down with intense pressure, but Chais wouldn't give up. He strained to lift his head up, slid his arms across the dirt to near his shoulders, and then used his strength to push himself upward. He had trouble holding his head up, but managed to slide a knee to his chest. He slumped on his knee for a second to catch his breath, then continued his struggle.

In about a minute, he managed to stand, wobbly at that, but still standing. And when he lifted his head, he noticed how badly off Earth actually was. All he could see were ruins. Collapsed buildings and crushed streets and vehicles—all rusted or decayed. No plants were in view—only the site of black, gray, and brown destruction.

"Welcome to the metropolis of Greenwood," Vecto said in reference to the old name for the city. "I'm surprised you can stand. A human would have died due to the lack of blood to the brain. But I guess Zendorians are a bit stronger."

Chais ignored that comment. "You … said Earth was full of life," he commented instead, trying to regulate his breathing. He could see Vecto now and noticed that he no longer had the image of Robert Newman that he became so accustomed to. Instead, Vecto had the body of some robot with melted metal, as if acid had burned through it.

"Was," Vecto emphasized. "And I told you it was destroyed."

"Didn't think this much."

"I'm sorry to disappoint," Vecto mocked. He was sitting on some rubble, having waited on Chais to stand. He jumped off the rubble and turned around. "The Nagora clan is this way."

Chais slowly moved his body around, being careful not to fall. But he stopped in bewilderment when he saw the horizon, his knees shaking only because of the gravity. Reaching possibly into outer space as far to the sides as he could see was a curved wall of gray matter.

"Either my eyes are deceiving me or that's one heckuva huge wall."

Vecto realized what he was referring to. "Correction: it's the moon."

Chais arched an eyebrow. "You gotta be kiddin' me!" He looked more intently at the site. There were the craters—he could see them through the haze.

"When the Zadeross giants multiplied Earth's gravity with their gravity manipulation weapons, the moon was sucked in and crashed in the Atlantic Ocean," Vecto explained. "It left the planet blackened with dust for ages. Fortunately, Earth has planetary air generators—not enough to clear all the dust in the air, but enough to stabilize a breathing atmosphere."

"Man, I feel sorry for the humans," Chais said.

"Its impact made little difference. The surface of Earth was already destroyed due to the usage of the Omnipotous Bomb, a weapon highly combustible with oxygen. Fortunately, Acaterra was constructed by then and most people had already transferred there due to the eminent danger of the bomb."

"Then how did the Nagora clan survive?"

"With modified bodies. They essentially feed off of Zero Point Energy now because there's hardly any life left on the planet. But they're working on that. They made a forest of plants altered to live through Earth's new conditions. That's where we're headed." Vecto motioned for Chais to follow him. "An old friend of mine and former Alpha Squad member, Shadow, is now the leader of the clan. If there's anyone who knows the history of the Nagora clan and whether a clan member landed on planet Zendora, it would be him."

Vecto had to wait for Chais. The Zendorian painstakingly walked five miles or so into the city and was beginning to adapt to the gravity. Vecto noticed his adaption as well. He assumed Chais would get only weaker and more exhausted as they went on, but it was quite the opposite.

"I think I can go without support," Chais said in

reference to his sword that he leaned on as a prop. "I look like some old man. Besides, how long is it going to take to get there?"

"Ten hours at current pace. The clan is located east of the city in the wooded area."

"That long?! Well at least there's some life to this planet."

"On second analysis, I can attract the Nagora clan rather than make you take the hike," Vecto suggested.

"I'm game," Chais said, resting his hands on his knees as he bent over, sweat dripping from his face. He watched the perspiration smash to the concrete below. They were walking on an old broken-up road that was fitted with now-defunct magnetic rails to support old hovering vehicles.

Chais slowly turned his head to see Vecto pointing his gun over him, charging a Zero Point Energy beam.

"Stay down," Vecto said, then fired the blast.

Chais dropped to his knees as the blast zipped by and struck a half-collapsed skyscraper far in the distance. He looked up see a plume of smoke and dust swell from the destroyed site.

"What in blazes you doin'!"

"Attracting the ninjas," Vecto said. He walked over to some nearby rumble and sat down. "They'll be here in a matter of minutes."

Chais watched as the smoke lifted in the air. "Good, then I get that much time to train before they ambush us for destroying things."

Chais wasn't joking. He lifted his ex-cane of a sword from the ground with both hands, extended its blade, and swung it upward against the gravity. He swung again and again, each with more force, then let the gravity send the sword crashing to the surface.

"Guess I can lose the dead weight," Chais murmured to himself.

Vecto had watched how pathetically slow Chais moved under high gravity and pondered how much assistance he'd actually be against Morphaal. But Chais eased Vecto's doubts when he removed his trench coat.

Peeling the thick coat from his body, Chais grasped it by one hand and let it drop to the surface. It sounded like a ton of weight crashing to the surface. Chais tilted his head and popped his neck, then rolled his shoulders back and popped his ribcage. More bone popping followed as Chais quickly snatched his sword from the ground, grinded it out from the surface at an angle and slashed upward in the air with it, jumping several feet in the air in the process.

Vecto was impressed by his quick turnaround. "Reminds me of my friend Phantom," he said. "He used to wear a weighted cloak."

"I blame it on all the gadgets. It can add up."

"So why didn't you take the coat off when you first got here?"

"What? And leave it behind? I would have had to carry it anyway. Besides, I wouldn't have let you carry it."

"Thanks a lot," Vecto said sarcastically. He then diverted his attention to something else as Chais took his practice swings. His Lapton map picked up two figures standing on a couple of buildings.

"Sorry to cut your training short, but they're here."

"Already? I don't see anyone."

"Oh, by the way, they can turn invisible so to speak."

"Great. Now ya warn me."

Vecto gazed at the location of a ninja on top of ruins

and projected his voice to him. "I'm here to meet your leader, Shadow. I'm an old friend of his."

"I'm right here," a voice said in front of Vecto.

"Where?" Chais asked instead. He was expecting to see a glossy outline of a person caused by a cloaking device, but there was no such thing.

Vecto's scans couldn't pick up anyone in front of him, either, but he saw the shadow of a person ripple across rocks. It was Shadow, all right. Not only was he manipulating light to go around him, but he bent all wavelengths, including the ones Vecto used to scan his surroundings—a trick Shadow learned some time ago.

"You left your shadow," Vecto pointed out.

"It's my calling card," Shadow's voice responded. "It gets the ladies all the time."

"Do I look like a woman to you?" Vecto cut back.

Shadow laughed. In a flash, his image appeared. Chais was startled to see that Shadow had no cloak around him, nor was his face covered up to do the trick. Instead, what he saw was a man in his forties with a receding hairline wearing black pants and a white shirt with the slogan, "If seeing is believing, then I don't exist."

Chais glanced at Vecto. "Are you sure this is him? I mean, I thought he was some kind of ninja."

"It's my day off," Shadow said. "On a date, as a matter of fact, when I saw the smoke plume." He looked at Vecto. "You gotta have some balls coming here and destroying things."

"I came to get information on Morphaal's whereabouts," Vecto cut to the point. "I found out he's likely on a planet in the innerverse called Zendora and heard that members of the Nagora Clan crashed on the planet some time ago. I'm trying to find the coordinates to the planet and thought your people may have record of it."

"Hmm, so the rumor's true that Morphaal's back," Shadow mused. "I thought we got rid of him for good."

"Same here. Now about Zendora—"

"Never heard of it," Shadow abruptly responded. "If one of our clan members landed on the planet, he never returned. We wouldn't have specifics unless we had access to the ship's logs."

"No." Vecto shook his robotic head. "Maybe they sent out their location when they crashed."

"Sorry, Vec, I just don't know."

Vecto clutched his fist. Chais picked up on this and stepped away, deciding to stay mum.

"But I have to find Zendora! I have to find Morphaal!" Vecto yelled.

Shadow slightly squinted. "Heard you wreaked havoc on Acaterra—became tabloid fodder and surpassed Morphaal on the most-wanted list."

"I overreacted," Vecto admitted. "But I'm not here for a fight."

"I didn't mention a fight. But now that you mention it, you seem a little restless."

"What do you expect? I've exhausted nearly all of my resources to find Morphaal," Vecto said. "I'm supposed to have one of the most highly sophisticated programming, yet I can't find him. I hate not knowing things."

"I can beat you, Vecto," Shadow bragged.

"What?" Vecto was taken aback by the remark. Chais was curious as well.

"In fact, I've already won."

"Look, I've had to fight enough people and robots as it is," Vecto said. "I don't want to fight you. I came only for information."

To be on the safe side, Vecto commanded his shield to expand over his robotic body. He had lowered his shields when he was transported to Earth because the shields were feeding off his metallic body too much. He now realized he should have left the shields up—because his FFS wouldn't budge. Vecto noticed that Shadow had mentally formed Zero Pont Energy around his Flummox Capacitor orb. Shadow was keeping it from expanding and was suffocating it.

Vecto glanced back at Shadow. "Why?"

"You've got quite the price on your head," Shadow said. He looked at Chais, who was gradually raising his sword. "And if I were you, I'd leave this planet."

"What are you doing to him?!" Chais demanded as he pointed the blade.

"Oh, you still want to fight?" Shadow taunted.

Suddenly, missiles came at Shadow from Vecto, and all Chais could see were flashes of light and explosions. But the explosions weren't at Shadow. Chais slid back and covered his face as robotic parts jettisoned from Vecto, one cutting his arm. When he opened his eyes, Vecto's body was in pieces—all that was left was his orb.

"Geez! What just happened?" Chais yelled, still unsure if this was real. Did Shadow just defeat Vecto in a matter of seconds?

"Kid, I deflected the missiles back at him," Shadow responded, "with my sword."

Chais shook his head, speechless. Shadow would have had to use the side of his katana to curve each one of the missiles around—and he did it in seconds. Chais tightened his grip on the handle of his sword.

"Come on now—what are you starin' at? Leave already!" Shadow ordered.

Chais watched Vecto's orb lifelessly roll into some scrap metal. "You—you just took him out like nothin'!"

"Yeah, so—I know him—know him all too well," Shadow said, sliding his sword back in its sheath. "He's nothing without his shields. You've gotta strike first—when he's not expecting it. It's the only way you'll win against him."

Shadow noticed Chais didn't budged—neither did his sword. "You really want to fight? A friend of Vecto's to the death, huh?"

Chais smirked. "Not really. You see, I needed his help to beat Morphaal so I can collect some bounty, but I've got a change of plans."

Shadow was curious and listened.

"You said Vecto was higher on the hit-list than Morphaal," Chais continued. "Which means if I take you down and cash in on Vecto, then beat Morphaal, I'll be set for quite some time."

Shadow couldn't help but laugh. "You—you think you can beat Morphaal? And on top of that—me? You're delusional!"

"Without that surprise attack, you couldn't beat Vecto. You said it yourself," Chais said. He stuck the sword in the road and gripped the upside-down handle. "Well I've got some surprises of my own!"

Chais quickly dashed for Shadow, drug his blade in the concrete, and then slashed it upward. Shadow dodged the blade and wacked Chais in his wide-open side with his sheath.

But Chais switched the direction he held his sword and used the gravity to his advantage, coming down with the blade with both arms as if he was stabbing him with an oversized knife.

Shadow spun around to the back of Chais and jabbed the end of his sheath into him. Chais stumbled forward and ended up jabbing his sword into concrete.

"So you want to beat me so you can cash in on Vecto instead, huh?" Shadow remarked, hovering his hand around the handle of his katana. "Some friend!"

"You're one to talk!" Chais yelled back, coming at him.

"There's more to it than that," Shadow said, dodging Chais' random swings and kicking him in the chest.

Chais fumbled back a few feet. He needed his trench coat, but it was a few yards away. If only he could move the fight enough to reach it, he could make use of some of his gadgets.

Chais heard a swish and felt a gush of wind but didn't even see Shadow budge.

Shadow had his hand on the handle of his katana. He stood in front of Chais, watching as a diagonal slash mark appeared on a ruined building far behind Chais. He tilted his head to the side as the whole corner of the building slid off the rest of the building from the cut, crashing to the surface.

Chais looked back in enough time to witness the cut section explode into pieces. He could see strands of his hair twirling in the air away from him. That's when he realized that Shadow had slashed at him, missed him on purpose and sent energy from his blade into the building. It was a warning.

"OK. So you're good," Chais said. "Not as good as—"

He couldn't get the words out of his mouth when Shadow kicked him in the chest, sending him flying toward the destruction as if he was a human cannonball.

Chais crashed through the building that was sliced and ended up in a pile of debris against a wall. He stood up but several shurikens tagged his shirt and stuck him against the wall. In front of him stood Shadow.

"Hmm, your body's tougher than I thought," Shadow commented.

Chais yanked away from the wall, ripping his shirt off in the process. He stood there with a six-pack and pieces of torn clothing hanging from both arms.

"Whoa!" Shadow said. "Keep your shirt on, man! I'm only after the chicks!"

"You're ticking me off!" Chais yelled, grabbing his sword nearby and lunged at Shadow.

Shadow used his sheath to block the strikes, then struck Chais in the chest with it. Chais stumbled some more.

"Your hands aren't steady," Shadow critiqued his swordplay.

Chais swung his sword in place while detaching the blade. Shadow heard the sound of chains rattle above him. The blade struck a wall behind and Chais was reeled in by chains. As he was yanked up, he reached in his pants' pocket and tossed a bomb at Shadow.

Shadow jumped back as it exploded, shielding his face.

"Why you—" Shadow yelled. He quickly spun around and removed his katana. A slash of energy sliced the bottom half of the wall that Chais was now propped on. It caused the wall to collapse—Chais with it.

Consequently, the whole building crumbled. Shadow jumped up, slicing his way to freedom as the entire structure caved in. He forced his way through it as the final pieces settled, and he dropped down on top. There was only a heap left were the building once stood, and it buried Chais with it.

Shadow looked at his feet amidst the dust. The kid was

probably dead. "You did it to yourself. I told you to leave," Shadow mumbled.

The kid almost made him lose his concentration on Vecto. He had left Vecto's orb behind—still encompassed in energy.

"Master, do you still require our presence?" a voice said. It was one of Shadow's trainees, bowing before him. Next to him was his companion.

"Did you two learn anything?" Shadow asked.

"You fight well," the other ninja said, hidden in black wraps used by the clan.

"I showed you what not to do," Shadow said, shaking his head. "He wasn't an enemy. He didn't deserve to die. Now leave me alone."

"Yes, master," the two said in unison and disappeared.

Shadow looked down at the rubble one last time, somewhat regretting the outcome. But it wasn't his fault, he convinced himself.

He wasted no more time retrieving Vecto's orb. He stood hunched over the chrome-gray orb, noticing the small crater formed around it. He lifted it and turned to claim Chais' trench coat. But there was a guy wearing it. It was Chais.

"You didn't think you'd get rid of me that easily, did you?" Chais said adjusting the coat he just put on.

"But I just buried you …"

"Yeah, well, I had some teleporter thing-a-ma-jig in my pocket," Chais explained, scratching his head. "Borrowed it from a Dinishman."

Shadow smirked. "So you're full of tricks, huh? Me, too. You gonna leave now?"

"Why? And miss all the fun?"

Shadow grinned. He didn't bother to reply. His arms

went missing instead.

Chais witnessed Shadow's arms disappear. It was bizarre. They just vanished. No blood, no screen trick. The limbs were there one second and gone the next—taking Vecto's orb with it.

"Man, that's creepy!"

"You see, I can do a lot of tricks by manipulating light waves," Shadow explained.

Chais took notice of Shadow's sheath and could see his blade magically sliding from it, slowly disappearing as it was removed.

Shadow approached him.

"Now, we can do this the hard way or the brutal way," Shadow warned.

"Not much of a choice," Chais said, extending his blade. In a fraction of a second, he felt wind ripple by, followed by a sting trailing down his bare chest. He looked down to see blood trickle from a cut on his skin, then looked back at Shadow.

"OK, that's it!" Chais yelled. He quickly snatched an orb from within his coat and crushed it with his hand.

Shadow appeared still, but he was actually slashing with his katana. The strikes wouldn't hit Chais, though. They were clashing with an invisible field. It was a magnetic field that Chais created by crushing that orb. It repelled the blade's metal.

It gave Chais enough time for him to study Shadow. There—his shoulder blade—it twitched. Chais dropped his shield and lunged his sword at Shadow but clashed with an invisible object in front of Shadow's face.

Shadow's arms reappeared, as well as Vecto's orb. Chais' sword was against the orb.

"You're lucky he still has some shield left," Shadow

commented. "Not long before it suffocates." He then completely disappeared.

In reflex, Chais shifted his eyes to look for him. He quickly grabbed another orb from his coat and threw it to the ground, jumping back. Purple smoke fumed in the air and solidified, but Shadow wasn't there. Chais glanced around, caught the glimpse of purple particles coming at him and blocked a sword. Some of the particles had attached to Shadow's body and sword. Chais could at least pinpoint him.

Shadow realized this and returned to visibility. "Clever. Now how about this trick?"

Suddenly, it was pitch dark. Chais couldn't see a thing. Shadow blocked the light to his eyes.

"Man, you're good, I gotta admit," Chais said.

He felt the sting of Shadow's katana cut his chest again. He stumbled back, trying to focus his hearing on Shadow. This time he was cut in the arm, then the other arm. He had to think of something—fast!

He went for a slash and could hear the metal clash of Shadow's blade blocking it. He jumped back and paused. "All right, all right! I give!" Chais yelled. "I'll go home."

His eyesight returned and he saw Shadow standing before him. Shadow smirked, then sheathed his sword.

"Hey, you know, you're not cuttin' to kill—I respect that," Chais said, dropping his sword and raising his hands. "You won! I got it, I'll leave."

It was a bit abrupt for Shadow. He was having fun but he shrugged anyway and urged him on with a wave of his hand. "Good. Now don't come back."

"Whatever you say," Chais said.

Shadow nodded and disappeared. He then reappeared on a pile of rubble, staring at the moon in the distance. It was a victory for him, yet he was unsatisfied. Most people he battled to the death, but this kid was different. Perhaps he knew his limits—knew he couldn't win and gave up knowing it would have gotten more brutal the longer they fought. Perhaps the kid wanted to survive so he could plan a sneak attack later and retrieve Vecto's orb.

Shadow paused. He was missing the orb! He looked back to see Chais hustling away and cursed himself. "You little thief!!"

He disappeared and ran for Chais. He sped to him and with a quick strike from the sheath of his katana, smacked him in the back of the skull. Chais tumbled across the concrete. His body flopped around as Vecto's orb rolled away. The kid wasn't moving.

Shadow reappeared and grabbed the orb—forming energy back around it. The kid had managed to steal the orb, even when he was blinded. How was that possible? He must have stored it in the back of his coat to hide it. Clever. He stepped over to Chais and picked his body up. *He'll wake up soon*, he thought, carrying him off.

09

Morphaal's throne room was ahead. The images of Vecto, Gyro, Phantom, and Shadow stood behind a black wall in stealth.

"My scans indicate there are only two guards," Vecto said, shielding the floating parts of his robotic body.

"The-then I can take him," Gyro offered, his black body blending with the wall.

"Arr, we go together!" Shadow said—a bit too loud. Only his eyes were visible through the camouflage ninja garment over his head.

"Ah, contraire," Phantom interrupted, flinging his cloak. "It will be ideal if Shadow eliminates the goons while invisible as Vecto disables the cameras."

Erich Botland, as Vecto, concurred. He had played the virtual reality simulation game, A.S. Scape, before and knew if they were caught, their surprise attack would be foiled.

It seemed that Cutlass, playing as Shadow, agreed, despite Trip's (Gyro's) objections. And it also seemed that

Dr. Azmeck was quite the expert in the game as Phantom. He invited him to fill the fourth player spot but had no idea he would accept and be so good at it.

Following Phantom's advice, Shadow's body faded into invisibility.

The guards stood erect, watching their vicinity. One guy sneezed and the other said, "Hey, Carl." But when the other guard glanced back at him, blood flung up the guard's chest as a slash mark appeared on his body. The man was caught off guard by the brutal, spontaneous act and fired randomly at the falling, dead companion in hopes of hitting the invisible culprit. But in a whoosh, the air appeared to sever his gun hand, spun his body around, and sliced his throat.

"These bilge-sucking milksops are down, me hearties," Shadow called out.

"Camera's are down, too," Vecto said.

The Alpha Squad rushed to the gigantic sealed door. Gyro picked up the severed hand and placed his finger on the finger print recognition panel. His body began to shift, and Gyro reshaped his head into the face of the guard for the retina scan.

"Requesting access," Vecto said for Gyro in the dead guard's voice.

A few seconds passed before a robotic voice responded. "Access denied. All entry is prohibited."

"Ya-you gotta be ki-kiding me!" Gyro said, smashing his fist in the panel.

Alarms blared.

"Oh, great!" Vecto said. "It's gonna be game over for us now. That door's reinforced with tyrannium, and my scans are being blocked from detecting what's inside."

"Allow me," Phantom said, backing up. "Stand back if

you will." He rushed at the door and his body faded. He went intangible, phasing through the door, but came back through moments later.

"I took the liberty to clear the hallway," Phantom said amidst the alarm, "but the door won't open from the inside either. Vecto, use your Air-to-Ice to weaken the structure. Gyro, form your energy within it and expand it to clear an entrance."

The group nodded, and following Phantom's instructions, Vecto fired rapid shots of carbon ice at the door as Gyro focused to form a ball of energy within. Valignium, aka tyrannium, metal was odd in that its particles scatter and melt when subjected to extreme cold and solidify when hot. The zero point energy ball grew as the valignium melted. The energy exploded, creating a hole in the massive door, big enough for them to squeeze through.

They were at the end of the game. It was the final showdown with Morphaal. The Alpha Squad soon gathered at Morphaal's throne. The obese, nine-foot-tall cyborg was waiting for them. He clicked a button on his bloody, dark throne chair to seal the exits and calmly stood.

"Only four," Morphaal said as he walked down the steps, "four of the most potent beings in the universe, here to fight one man. I believe four is not enough."

"Ya-ya-you'll see otherwise!" Gyro yelled.

"Ah, but I differ," the game's A.I. of Morphaal responded. "I have allowed you four to strengthen. It was always my plan to kill you, each at your prime, all today."

Start forming the Giga Ball! Vecto said in Gyro's head. *We'll hold him off!*

"Charge, me hearties!" Shadow yelled a battle cry. He

rushed to Morphaal and swung his katana at his body as Morphaal descended the stairs, but Morphaal wasn't fazed. He grabbed Shadow's arm and crushed it. Shadow's sword dropped as Morphaal grabbed his forehead, lifted him, and began sucking energy from his body.

A zero point energy blast shot from Vecto's Blaster 3000, but Morphaal reached his other hand out, grabbed it, and sucked that energy as well.

In a flash, Phantom disappeared and reappeared on the steps—crouched with Shadow's sword in his hand. Energy burst in the air from Morphaal's arm after Phantom sliced it, but he didn't drop Shadow. Instead, Morphaal hurled Shadow toward Gyro.

Vecto rushed and grabbed Shadow before he struck him, then released two Foot Missiles. They couldn't use normal energy attacks. But his missiles could do the trick.

Two massive explosions engulfed the large room as Phantom went intangible and as Vecto formed a shield over Gyro and Shadow.

But the smoke cleared, and Morphaal was in the same spot, barely scathed, hovering in the air. He dropped to the destroyed steps, pounding his sheer weight on it, causing the surface to rumble and dust to scatter.

"Pathetic!" he said. He looked over his mechanical body as lumps of energy blistered on him like leeches. Gyro focused, forming the energy onto Morphaal's body. Suddenly, Phantom blurred by, striking the energy lumps with his sword to blow them up as he passed.

Morphaal stumbled but only sustained minor cuts and dents to his armor.

It was Vecto's turn. He appeared and pounded his fist into Morphaal's chest. The cyborg stumbled again but laughed.

Morphaal blasted a sphere of energy around him, knocking Vecto out of the way. Sharp energy beams shot from the barrier, rotating omni-directionally. The A.S. shielded themselves and dodged as the white beams scattered like a strobe light.

"How's that Giga Ball coming," Vecto asked Gyro with his shields protecting him. Gyro didn't have to answer. Vecto changed his vision mode to see the invisible energy all around them, with a tiny visible core in front of Gyro's chest.

Morphaal dropped his energy attack and glanced at the A.S.

"Ga-ga-game over!" Gyro yelled. He leaped over Shadow and came down on Morphaal. His clutched fist unraveled, and he shoved the tiny Giga ball into Morphaal's chest.

Morphaal knocked Gyro back and looked down at his pierced body armor. The energy was digging through his breastplate.

Then the game blackened.

Trip, Cutlass and Azmeck were disconnected from the virtual game. Where was the ending? Where were the credits? Did they beat the game?

They could hear yells in the background as they took off their A.S. Scape devices latched beside their eyes.

"Put your hands up!" a Coronan guard yelled at someone. "Now get down on the ground!"

The person complied as Trip, Cutlass and Azmeck stood from their seats, bewildered as to what was happening. The crowd of frantic spectators in the arcade room made it hard for them to see what was transpiring. But they managed to get a glimpse of the suspect. They could see Erich. He stood, his hands cuffed as the guards escorted him away.

* * *

It had been a week since Vecto was defeated. He could finally hear and see now—which meant his shields were back. The first thing he saw was Shadow starring at him as if he was some new specimen. Vecto realized he was in an energy containment field.

"Vecto, I had to do this," Shadow said.

The strange thing was Vecto wasn't mad at him. He thought back to his fight with Streamline. He was foolish to think Streamline was betraying him when he was actually saving him. It took Crysilis to interfere for him to understand. And he knew Shadow long enough to know that money was meaningless to him on old Earth. There was a reason Shadow defeated him. He knew him all too well.

"Vecto," Shadow called out. "If you can hear me, I'd like to explain."

"Go ahead," Vecto said.

"You see, Acaterra has been in turmoil ever since the Alpha Squad was branded as an enemy," Shadow explained as he sat in a chair beside Vecto's orb. "When Streamline turned himself in and gave them your robotic body, I knew he didn't give them your orb. The government found out, too, but played along with their story that you were defeated to make themselves look good. Didn't want a PR disaster."

He waited for Vecto to say something, but when he didn't, he went on. "But the truth spread like wildfire—people found out about the cover-up. A revolution quickly formed. Somehow, someone had smuggled a shipload of weapons on Acaterra and distributed them through the black market. People were scared that if you were still alive, they needed to defend themselves because the government sure wasn't helping. But, more importantly, the working class took that opportunity to form a coalition against the Acaterran government."

Vecto was familiar with the social system of Acaterra. Almost every job was government-run and commission-based. The working class made ends meet and the leisure class was paid to spend to keep the economy going. Riots usually didn't go far because their livelihood depended on the government. But with weapons added to the equation, it painted a whole different picture of what might happen.

"There have been a number of assassination attempts on government officials—some successful. The government thinks you were the root cause for this chaos and have upped the wager on your destruction."

"So to cut to the point, you were being watched," Vecto said.

"Clever as always." Shadow smirked. "They've been spying on me since with satellites, waiting to see if you'd contact me. I saw a sniper about five miles from you, too, when I rushed to the scene."

"Don't worry, it was Accura. She's on her own. I'm letting her stalk me."

"Oh, so it's a chick?" Shadow asked. "And you didn't introduce me?"

"The story?"

"Yeah, yeah. Well, you see, I had to make it look like you were destroyed."

"I know," Vecto responded. "That's why I fired the missiles."

Shadow cocked an eyebrow. "Then why am I explaining all this?"

"I knew something was wrong when you suffocated my shields," Vecto said. "And I assume you kept me in this underground facility of yours for good cause."

"Yeah, had to make sure they couldn't pick up any waves from you, or whatever you emit," Shadow explained. "The satellite's passed by now. But there's something else. About Zendora."

Vecto was silent.

"I looked up the records and there was a ship that got lost in the innerverse a few hundred years ago while exploring. It was a joint project our clan was doing when Acaterra was in construction. The good news is we've got the ship's identification code. The bad news is we don't have the coordinates."

Vecto figured as much.

"But Acaterra does. The ship emitted its location with a distress call."

It was the best news Vecto had heard in a long time. "So it took a few hundred years before we received the signal," Vecto said, knowing that the ansible wasn't invented yet. Faster-than-light communication wasn't possible at the time, and it couldn't just travel in wormholes like their ships could.

"Right," Shadow confirmed. "If you can look up the ship's code, you can find its last location. I couldn't tell you before while being watched. And if what Chais says is true about clan members crashing on Zendora, it's probably them. But this means you'll have to go back to Acaterra."

"No," Vecto disagreed. "There's one other place. So where's Chais?"

"Been training him since. Good kid. Come on. He's eat'n breakfast," Shadow said. He flipped a switch to shut down the field around Vecto's orb and waved for him to follow.

Vecto formed the image of Robert Newman and followed Shadow to the dance club.

"Yo, you awake now, huh?" Chais yelled to Vecto overtop the blaring techno music. He took a bite out of his breakfast wrap as multi-colored lights flashed around the room. "You know, I thought these ninjas would be living in tents and all, but I guess they're pretty cool after all."

"I'm leaving," Vecto said.

"Aw, come on. You just woke up. Have some fun. Do a robot dance or somethin'." Chais swallowed the rest of his wrap and performed a choppy dance Vecto could do.

"I'm going back to the Corona,' Vecto said. "I need to talk to Sarah again."

"Who?" Chais yelled. "You mean you got yourself a chick? Way to go, man!"

"Obviously, Shadow's rubbing off on you," Vecto mumbled.

"What!" Chais couldn't hear him.

"I'm leaving. Follow if you want."

Chais stopped dancing. "But I'll go back to jail."

"Are you worried?"

Vecto returned to Hodos. Fortunately, Shadow had a teleportation station in his underground home. It was getting dark on Hodos as he walked toward the Corona. He knew nightfall wouldn't last long. With two stars, the planet was almost always lit, even if it didn't get much heat. It didn't bother Vecto. He had his Robert Newman image on as he paced through the planet's unusual mud. The view of the colossal human ship grew closer with each heavy step. And in front of it were several Coronan guards, a Magnatronian, and Chais.

The Magnatronian tossed Chais into a Coronan guard,

who then grabbed Chais by his trench coat.

"Hey, let go of me, you punk!" Chais yelled at the guard.

"Shut up!" the Coronan guard said as he yanked Chais by the back of his trench coat. The guard cuffed Chais' hands with magnetic disks. "You're under arrest. It's back to the brink for you, buddy!"

The Magnatronian starred at the Coronan guard in hatred and walked off. The Terrans were still enemies to him.

A chill ran through the guard's body, but he shook it off and pushed Chais to move.

The other guards noticed a man wearing a red suit approaching.

"Thank goodness ya'll caught him," Vecto said. "He took me off the ship and tried to use me for ransom."

It took another glance for the Coronan guards to recognize him.

They swiftly snapped their guns in place. "Put your hands in the air!" they yelled, followed by the same reaction of other guards. His description matched the police report, all right. It was the guy wanted on murder charges.

It wasn't what Vecto planned. Perhaps they discovered him. Perhaps Accura told them his identity after all. "Is there a problem?" he asked, lifting his arms.

"Get down on the ground!" yelled one guard as he shuffled to him with his gun steady.

Vecto complied and dropped to his knees. He didn't want to make a scene and blow his cover if they didn't know he was Vecto. Slowly, he put his hands behind his back as an armored guard placed cuff magnets on his wrist. Vecto let them "attach" to him and magnetize together to lock his arms.

"Can you tell me what's wrong?" Vecto questioned.

The guard pushed Vecto to stand. "You're wanted on criminal charges of first-degree murder of Coronan guards and prisoners, aiding a criminal in escape, use of a firearm in a criminal act, trespassing on governmental property, unlawful entry, fleeing from a crime scene, traveling without a passport, leaving a transport ship without permission and fleeing from Coronan officers," the guard informed him as he shoved him to move. Fortunately, his thick armor kept him from feeling any sting from Vecto's shields.

Vecto had to think of a new plan.

The crime scene was bloody a week ago. The bodies of guards, soldiers, and prisoners were removed from the sealed prison block, but bloodstains were scattered below holographic images of the victims, used by forensics. Investigators pinpointed the suspects down to three people: Erich, Chais, and Vecto. Chais had escaped from prison, Vecto was seen near the prison facility with a stolen cross in his hand, and Erich was seen with him. All were near or at the crime scene before video footage was corrupted. All had motive.

Erich was interrogated first. The Corona investigators thought he turned in the pirates he fought as a cover-up-to look like a good guy. He kept them alive due to the bounty he would receive. When Rob Newman offered a price to retrieve a confiscated cross and eliminate any witnesses, Erich accepted. He killed the guards and prisoners, retrieved the cross, and let Chais go free as a scapegoat. Erich was a bounty hunter, after all.

Then Chais was interrogated after being captured. They

believed he lured a guard to his cell, snatched his gun, killed some guards, freed himself, and killed the prisoners to eliminate any witnesses. He made a deal with Rob in exchange for the cross and fled from the ship onto Magnatronian territory to avoid being caught.

Lastly, Rob was interrogated. They had combat footage of him fighting the pirates, thought he had an animosity toward them, and understood he had an attachment to the stolen cross. They believe he went to the prison facility to retrieve the cross, disabled the cameras, and killed the pirates—killing the guards in his way. He stole the cross but let Chais escape to blame the incident on him.

When interrogations were complete, Vecto and Erich were released but given a monitor—in hopes that new evidence would surface.

Vecto and Erich returned to their bunks. Erich's tracker looked like an oversized mole, one he couldn't remove without causing nerve damage. It made no difference to Vecto, but he kept his on. When they walked into the room, Trip and Cutlass bombarded them with questions such as why they were arrested, or where had they been for the past week? Erich and Vecto kept their answers short. They explained that they were suspects because they were in the area at the time of the killings and both said they were innocent. Erich explained he was detained for so long as a precaution. Vecto said he was taken hostage off the ship but managed to come back.

The conversation eventually shifted.

"So-so what do you do for a living?" Trip asked Vecto.

"I have a libertarian show," Vecto replied as he sat down on the bottom bunk. At least that's what Drew, the worker at the waste-to-energy processing plant, said a week ago when he had recognized him.

"Aaarrr, a right fine job ye have," Cutlass added. "Ye need to watch those scurvy bilge rat government people. Those landlubbers gave me the boot."

"E-eno-enough with the 'aaarrr' already!" Trip scolded him. "Pirates don't say 'aaarrr,' and the ones today don't even speak like that!"

"Ye be jealous, me hearty?

Vecto interjected, "So why do you talk that way?"

"A pirate, I be. It be what I last remember, me buccaneer."

"He lost his m-memory," Trip answered for him. "I heard he wa-was in the military on m-my homeworld b-be-before it was attacked."

"What happened?" Vecto asked.

"Him? I don't know," Trip answered. "I ju-just got out of the orphanage again to a g-good foster home when my new parents were killed by the outsiders. I wa-was left on the streets when I met Cutlass. He sh-showed me where the homeless lived and w-where the food was, and I helped him stowaway on this ship."

"Who attacked your world?" Vecto asked, wondering if Morphaal was involved.

"Minions of s-someone who goes by the name Chaos," Trip replied. "Other th-than that, I don't know." Trip glanced up at Erich lying in the bunk above Vecto. "Are y-you OK, Erich? Y-you're not saying much."

Erich continued to stare at the glowing lights on the ceiling, his eyes following the energy streams to the door. "It's just, uh, it's just been a long week."

"W-well get some sleep," Trip said. "Don't worry about it." It was advice Trip had a hard time following. Sleep was scarce for him, partially due to Cutlass' snores and partially due to thinking too much. Besides, Rob gave him the creeps the last time he spent the night, like he was watching him.

"Yeah. Guess you're right," Erich said, then wished him goodnight.

Cutlass was already asleep, snoring.

In the morning, they awoke when the door opened. Coronan guards clad in armor stormed in the room, pointed their weapons, and shouted overdramatically, "Put your hands in the air! You're under arrest!"

They were pointing at Erich.

"What's going on?" Vecto asked.

"Put your hands in the air!" the guards ordered Erich.

Erich complied and Vecto got out of his bed to confront them.

"I asked what's going on!" Vecto demanded.

Cutlass and Trip kept quiet.

"Now climb down slowly," the guard ordered Erich and motioned for another guard to check the drawers between the beds.

The guard opened the top drawer and lifted a gun from it, then scanned it with his visor. "It's positive. It's the murder weapon we've been looking for."

"What? How did that get here?" Erich asked.

"You can drop the act," the lead guard said. "You've been found guilty of murder. We've deciphered the corrupted video, and it shows you committing the murders in the jailhouse. Now get down from that bunk, or I'll be forced to open fire!"

Erich complied as Trip and Cutlass sat in disbelief.

So they think he committed the murders, Vecto thought. This was his chance to find out if he was he the bounty hunter he was looking for, the one who bought Vic's robots.

"You're not taking him," Vecto said.

A couple guards pointed their guns at Vecto.

"Don't worry, Rob," Erich said. "I'll be OK." He lifted his arms for them to cuff him.

Vecto walked toward them. "Take me instead."

"We ain't got nothing on you, so be glad!" the lead guard said, motioning the guard to stand down. "Confiscate the armor," he said to the guard.

He cuffed Erich and escorted him out.

"E-Erich!" Trip called out.

"Be strong, me hearty!" Cutlass yelled.

Why would Erich go so willingly for a crime he didn't commit? Vecto thought. *Something's not right. Maybe Sarah knows.* He planned to reach her at a terminal this morning anyway. Might as well see what was actually going on.

"Hey guys, I'll be back," Vecto said.

"Wa-wait!" Trip said. "If y-you're going to do what I think you are, y-you'll be incarcerated, too!"

"Don't worry. I know someone who can help."

Vecto left and found a terminal. Sarah hadn't been answering her name in front of cameras, so he needed to reach her though the system.

"Sarah, it's me," he said through the terminal.

He didn't get a response.

"Sarah, it's Vecto. Come in."

Still no response.

Something really was wrong. He had no choice but to hack into her.

He touched the terminal and started his work. It was easier than he thought, as if Sarah allowed him access. He sifted through the files and came across the prison camera records. The videos showed Erich killing the guards. They showed Chais escaping afterward. Vecto then skipped to the storage room of robots and sped up the video. It showed Erich entering the room. But what about Sarah? He searched for her memory files but they were heavily encrypted. She was operational but not communicating. Maybe Dr. Azmeck knew something. He searched for his records and called him through the terminal. Fortunately, he answered.

"Dr. Azmeck," Vecto said. "Something is wrong. I can't reach Sarah."

"Hmm, is that so?" Azmeck said. The ship shook.

The ship must have been taking off. *But without Sarah?*

"Ah, feel that? There's your answer," Azmeck said. "You see, she's fine, lad. Only she can fly this ship."

"But she didn't warn the passengers."

There was a pause. "Indeed, she didn't." It was protocol to make an announcement, and Sarah was incapable of breaking orders. "Have you tried the command center?"

"It's my next stop."

"Then be quick at it," Azmeck said. "It may by the work of a certain bounty hunter."

"You mean the one who bought Master Vic's robots?"

"Afraid so."

Vecto disconnected the link.

"Erich … I trusted you," Vecto said, "You traitor!"

Erich was pushed into a brown prison cell occupied by an Asian-looking guy. It was Feit. "What are you doing here?" Erich asked.

"I could say the same about you, sir." Feit quipped. "I was caught trespassing on Magnatronian territory." He sat with his legs crossed as if in meditation.

"They put me in for a murder I didn't do," Erich said, shaking his head.

"Are you ... aren't you that guy who busted my nose?" a voice said from the cell beside them. "I know that voice."

Erich leaned closer to the wall between their cells. "Oh, great, you must be that TAC thief."

"Glad you two know each other," Feit said sarcastically.

"I'd rather be a thief than a murderer," Chais quipped back at Erich.

"Didn't you just hear me say I'm innocent?"

"That's what they all say," Chais said. "Who was it? A granny, or child? Whoever it was, she had to have been weak!"

Erich slammed his fist into the metal wall and blood trickled down from his knuckles. "I was framed! I swear I didn't kill any guards or prisoners!"

"Huh?" Chais said. "You mean the guy who did that killing spree in here? They're saying you did that?"

Erich lowered his head and heard Chais walk toward the wall.

"You've got to be kidding me!" Chais continued. "Your voice is much too whinny to be him!"

"You mean you heard him?"

"Yeah. Very calm soundin' while he shot 'em."

"Well can you tell the guards that and get me free?"

"Doubt they'd believe you," Feit inputted.

"Yeah, they claim to have video proof," Erich said, leaning his back against the wall. It had to have been altered. Someone must have hacked into the system. But who was capable of doing such a thing and why?

He slid down the wall until he sat on the cold metal

floor. He had to figure this crime out—not just to clear his name—but to save others from death. He should know enough about the murder as many times as he talked to the interrogator. He knew that all of the victims were shot in the forehead and that the sealed entrance was forced open from the inside by a sword. The murderer had to have come from the inside. He thought of Chais but shook the thought away. Or the murderer came in another way. He looked passed the bars at the center guard down the hall. He was standing about the spot where the first death occurred. If he were shot in the forehead, the bullet would have had to come from straight ahead. He looked up in thought. Or …

Erich quickly crouched and tilted his head up to look above the guard.

"What are you doing?" Feit asked.

"The guard was looking up! The murderer must have come in from above."

"You know, I did hear something over there. I never did hear the door open," Chais chimed in.

"What else," Erich pressed, walking closer to the wall to hear.

"Heard a shot, heard a struggle, then heard some more shots—a different sound, though," Chais explained. "What if he stole a guard's gun?"

"That could explain it."

"But what's strange is that he kept counting aloud. Counting after each shot. I jumped to the ceiling of my cell to hide; held myself up in the corner of the wall. The guy passed by each cell, killing everyone. Then the power went out. Hey, I won't complain. I was a free man."

"Where'd he go?"

"Back to the center. He must have gone back through the ceiling 'cause I didn't hear the door open."

"Are we ready to escape, then?" Feit calmly said, standing up. He feared the worse. What if it was Vecto, after all, counting each death. He could have easily rolled through a shaft and killed the guards and prisoners to retrieve Gyro's cross. He could have taken the form of Erich, as well.

"These bars are made of some nasty energy," Chais said.

"I'll take care of it," Feit said.

Erich stood in his way. "If I escape, then they'll really think I'm the murderer."

"Then it's settled, sir. I'll take you hostage," Feit said. "Blame it on me."

He concentrated with his hands in front of him and formed a ball of chi energy in between. He split the energy apart with his hand into smaller spheres and pushed each one against a laser prison beam. They went through them. He then stuck his hands in the middle of the energy and split them again—one down, one up—retreating the bar's lethal energy. It formed a gap to fit through.

"How did you—" Erich whispered. "Never mind. What about the guard?"

"I'll take care of him," Feit said. He grabbed a piece of sharpened chicken bone from dinner and stuck his head out from the bars. He flicked the bone at the guard, striking him in the neck. The guard grunted for just a moment before his body collapsed to the floor.

"All clear," Feit said.

"What about me?" Chais said in the other cell.

"Should I?" Feit asked Erich.

"I don't know," Erich said as he stepped through the gap. "You're the kidnapper."

"All right. We'll just blame it all on him."

10

As soon as Erich, Feit, and Chais stepped out of their cells, nothing out of the ordinary happened. Although Feit took care of the guard, they should have been under some sort of surveillance. There was nothing.

"I was expecting an alarm," Erich said. "I'm sure they're watching us."

"They want to see us escape," Feit explained. "I believe that since the door was opened by a sword last time, they assumed you got Chais to do it."

"Those thieves!" Chais yelled from afar, already in the storage room rummaging through items. "My weapons are gone!"

"They'd be fools to make the same mistake," Feit said. "I gather they're imprisoning us in a pod and have their men waiting outside that door. The cell wasn't our prison. The facility is."

"That explains the one guard," Erich said. "We need to hurry before they storm in."

"I sincerely doubt they're going to enter seeing that you

killed dozens of their men."

"But I didn't!" Erich corrected.

Feit laughed.

"Real funny." Erich slid a table in the center of the room and jumped on it to check the ceiling. "When I find the secret entrance, we can get out of here."

"Here, let me handle it," Feit said. He stepped over to a chair, lifted it with a foot, and tossed it up, kicking it at the ceiling. It missed Erich but caused a part of the ceiling to jolt.

"Hey, watch it!"

"Someone had cut through the ceiling and replaced it," Feit said. "Let's go."

Chais slapped his one-piece prison outfit. "I ain't leavin' without my weapons! Besides, I gotta get out of these tights."

"Suits me," Erich said. He slid the previously-cut square in the ceiling aside and lifted himself up into it. Feit followed.

"Hey, you're just gonna leave me?" Chais shouted. He walked over to the table and looked up at the hole. He then straightened the bent chair and sat in it. "Fine by me." He leaned back in the chair, looking at the time shining from a wall. He leaned back too far in the chair but grabbed the table as the chair slipped under him. At last, he stood up and walked to the entrance.

"Better now than never," he said, then clicked the button to open the door.

The space above the ceiling was a tight fit, but enough to crawl through. It was far from pitch-black, however, as blue-lit dust swirled from humming air generators, gleaming from the bright blue energy coursing throughout the ceiling shaft like a circuit board. The Zero Point Energy zigzagged throughout the ship in a grid, powering the ship.

"I thought Chais would've changed his mind after leaving him," Erich said as he and Feit crawled.

"Maybe he's scared of falling through," Feit said.

They heard gunshots from where they came from.

"Oh no! Chais!" Erich said. His voice echoed and Feit nudged him.

"Quiet. You'll give us away," Feit said. "Don't be fooled in thinking Chais is dead. He can handle himself."

"We need to go back!" Erich said, using his elbows and knees to turn around.

"Trust me. He's not the target."

"Yeah, I am," Erich mumbled. He shuffled around again. "Wait. I think I see a trail," Erich said, reaching his arm out to block Feit from advancing. He could see tracks through the dust that someone else made from crawling. "This way."

Following Erich's lead, they reached a vent at the end of the path. As they approached, they heard voices below, so they kept silent. Erich peeked through the vent to see a white laundry room filled with cylinder cleanser machines. In the room, two people were talking.

Erich gasped. Standing there was a tall man around twenty in a red and black powersuit that looked like flaming coal. He had long, rigid, red hair and held a hand towel.

I should have known, Erich thought to himself. He leaned his ear to the vent.

"And what about the pay?" an old woman said to the young one.

"In due time, my lovely lady. You deserve it. I

appreciate you putting my gun back in my room. I could've been caught with it in public."

"Aw, it was nothin', sweety. Just did a little housekeeping is all. So about the pay …"

"Shh," The red-haired man placed a finger on her lips, dangling the hand towel from his hand, then moved his hand behind her head. "I have another one."

He moved her head down so she could see what he had under the towel.

It was a single claw attached to the back of his glove.

Her eyes bulged and she screamed as he did an uppercut, stabbing her in the forehead, holding her head forward, caressing her as he yanked the blade out.

Erich looked away, panting, but he heard the woman's body thump to the ground. Feit was startled as well but didn't make a sound.

It was him all right. Erich looked back to see him lick the blood from the blade. He tossed the towel on the old woman's body and casually walked to a cleansing machine.

Erich clutched his fists, livid that another person had to die. She probably didn't even know it was a setup when she put the gun in Erich's drawer.

"Life is meaningless," Tyran said to himself. "A mere allusion." He clicked a button on the cylinder machine. "Death, however, is the only meaning we have. It is an inevitable outcome, a savior to this pathetic life."

Erich fumed up in the vent, unable to do anything but watch.

Tyran reached into the cylinder and pulled out a large armlet gun hidden within. He attached it to one arm, then took out two swords.

"My life was ruined by you," Tyran continued, attaching the swords to the back of his suit. "My existence discarded, scrap for the homeless pet. You will experience what I fear. No one will like you. Everyone will fear you. You will be forced to accept your identity, and it will destroy you."

He took out a needle and stabbed himself in the neck, injecting himself with some kind of substance. He growled in pain and his veins popped out.

"Heh heh heh!" He laughed hysterically. "Do you hear me, Erich!?"

Tyran looked up at the vent and Erich gasped. The next thing Erich knew, a blade stabbed through the vent before his eyes. The blade slashed across and pulled back out.

"Get back!" Erich yelled at Feit.

Tyran's claw stabbed through again. It sliced down beside them, creating a cutout. Erich and Feit tried to crawl away, but with one more slice to the ceiling, it collapsed. They tumbled down, landing below on the scrap of metal.

"Look what the cat dragged in," Tyran said, bending down and placing his claw at Erich's throat.

Feit leaped and kicked at Tyran's face, but Tyran caught his foot with his other hand and slung him into a nearby cleanser, keeping the claw at Erich's throat.

"Aaron! Stop this!" Erich pleaded.

"The name Aaron is dead. You will call me Tyran!" Tyran grabbed him by the throat and lifted him, slamming him into the wall. His hand closed tighter and he started to choke the life from him.

"Leave him alone!" Feit yelled. He recovered and punched Tyran's back. It pounded hard, but Tyran elbowed Feit in the face, not looking back.

"This is between me and him!" Tyran said.

"You killed the guards and prisoners, I assume," Feit said as he stood back up, wiping blood from his nose.

A slight laugh passed through his pale lips as he tilted his head to the side. "Oh, but of course. But I'm surprised Erich broke the law, too—escaping from jail … what a criminal." Tyran slowly turned around while holding Erich in the air by the throat. He kept his head low as shadows and strands of red hair casted over his eyes.

Erich struggled to breath. He grabbed Tyran and kneed him in the gut, but it didn't faze him.

"Fight him like a man!" Feit yelled.

Tyran laughed. He stabbed Erich in the shoulder with his claw, the blade piercing through the other side, then pulled it out as he threw him at Feit. Feit caught him, but they tumbled into a cleanser.

Erich gasped for fresh air and grabbed his shoulder.

"Are you OK?" Feit asked him.

Erich shook his head.

Feit stood up to face Tyran. "Why'd you do it?"

"The murders, you mean?" Tyran asked. "To frame Erich, naturally. And to eliminate those worthless pirates of mine."

Erich coughed. "So you were on their side?!"

"How else could I have gotten aboard?" He cocked his head in Erich's direction. "I'm head of the Blood Claw pirates, now—ever since you destroyed my life as a bounty hunter. You should have killed me when you had the chance!"

Erich stood up and stumbled closer, holding his shoulder. He was helpless without his suit, and Tyran knew it.

"Erich!" Feit said, stepping in the way.

"No. Let me handle this," Erich said, pushing him aside.

"You see," Tyran said, "that pirate attack was a distraction. They were just toying with you, is all. My main objective was to infiltrate this ship."

"Why? Just to frame me?" Erich asked.

"I locked you up to destroy your goody-two shoe name and to keep you from ruining my plans!"

Tyran raised his arm and fired from his armlet device. Feit yanked Erich away as a shell penetrated the cleansing machine and exploded. Shrapnel tossed overhead as Feit slid to the metal that had fallen from the ceiling and kicked it up. The piece intercepted another Explosion Shell and shattered. Feit then kicked a shard in midair at Tyran, but it was blocked by the side of Tyran's armlet gun. The piece stuck out from the armlet.

Tyran laughed. "Persistence is a graveyard!" He fired a shell at Feit, but Feit leaped forward. The floor exploded as Feit snatched the shard from Tyran's armlet, spun around, and stabbed him in the back with it.

Tyran leaned over, laughing.

Energy coursed through his blood-red suit, disintegrating the shard. A burst of energy emitted and pushed Feit back. Tyran's veins grew dark and his eyes turned blood red.

"No! No!" Tyran yelled, grabbing his head. "Stop it!"

Feit sat up from the ground, confused.

"Not yet. Not yet!"

"Aaron!" Erich yelled. "You need to control it!"

"Ahhg!" Tyran blindly lifted his arm and fired shots in the air, spinning his arm around, blasting walls and cleansing machines. Fire-extinguishing gas was released and automatic alarms blared.

Erich rushed to Feit's side but grunted in pain from his shoulder. "We need to get out of here!"

Without arguing, he followed behind, taking cover behind cleansers as they rushed to an exploded wall.

Tyran kept firing Explosion Shells until he ran out. He stood crouched over, panting. His eyes turned back to normal, and his blood calmed. He looked around, searching for Erich. He was gone.

"You will pay for my suffering!" Tyran yelled.

Vecto reached the ship's bridge and hit the entry button to get buzzed in. He had heard some explosions elsewhere on the ship, but he had to find Sarah first. Nobody came to the double doors, and there was no robotic voice to tell him he was not permitted to pass, so he entered the old-fashioned way—by jabbing his fist through it. Vecto used his shield to yank the doors apart and rushed in. It was what he feared and what his Lapton map revealed. There was no one in the room alive. Bodies lay, hanging from chairs, on the steps, and in the balcony.

He didn't have to scan them to see that they each were shot in the forehead. He didn't need his scanner to tell him they were the bridge crew, including Captain Tarcomed.

Vecto rushed to the terminal and tried again to contact Sarah. It was no good. Instead, he accessed video footage of what had happened and rapidly scanned it.

It was Erich committing the murders.

So it's true, Vecto thought.

"Freeze!" Coronan guards yelled at him.

"Holy Rama!" a guard gasped after seeing the captain dead.

"Get out of my way!" Vecto yelled, walking toward them.

"Stop right there!" a guard said.

Vecto kept coming so they opened fire. Bullets

ricocheted off Vecto's image of a body. A couple of the bullets even came back and struck them. Vecto pushed two of them out of the way, sending them to the far wall. Bullets struck Vecto's face but did nothing.

"What kind of freak are you?!" a guard asked, still firing.

Vecto ignored him and walked over to a door they sealed. He head-butted it to make an opening, then used his arms to pull it apart and go through it.

"Hull breach! Where's the hull breach button?" one of the guards yelled, scrambling to find it. He touched a section of the wall and it opened up. Then he smashed the emergency button. A thick door dropped down in front of Vecto, followed by one behind the door he demolished. The Coronan guards rushed to the sealed door.

"Subject is contained," the leader said through comlink in his helmet. "He's not human."

Another one switched on surveillance. They could see Vecto approach the wall and inspect the energy that streamed by to power the ship. They watched him punch it, particles of energy dispersing until the tube repaired itself. Vecto punched it again, this time holding his fist in it.

"What's he doing?" a guard asked.

Vecto formed a bubble with his shields to capture the energy and absorbed it until it filled the shield pocket. He removed his fist and compressed the shield bubble. The energy was harmless unless condensed. He packed the energy into a small ball and threw it at the transparent, metal-like glass on the hull. It exploded upon contact.

The guard stumbled back. "Subject has breached the hull!" he yelled. "He's outside the ship!"

The ship was exiting the atmosphere of Hodos. Vecto

stood on the ship as it sped through upper skies. Using his shield to keep him adhered to the hull, he ran on top of the ship as it cleared the atmosphere. He had to reenter the ship before it created a gravity well. The initial jolt could knock him off. He knew where to go—the passenger loading dock. At any time, Erich could activate the Viper robots in the holding bay. Vecto had to get there first.

Erich and Feit rushed through a frantic crowd to safety. Feit led him to the civilian docking bay and Erich rested against a wall, panting.

"What are we going to do?" Erich asked. "I need my suit to fight him!"

"We need a plan. And perhaps a powerful robot."

"What?"

Feit grabbed Erich by the shoulder but Erich cringed. He grabbed the other one in response. "Listen carefully. There's a robot on this ship named Vecto."

"Vecto!" Erich said. "He's on this ship?"

"Yes, sir. If we can get his attention, he can help us."

"And how do you suppose we reach him."

"I believe Vecto will be headed to this location."

"Fancy meeting you here," a voice said. It was Chais. He was wearing his cloak and had a backpack slung over his back.

"How did you—" Erich started to say.

"Escape?" Chais finished the question. "Let's just say I was trained by a ninja."

"And your weapons?"

"I told you I wasn't leaving without them."

"Did you bring my suit?" Erich asked.

"Yep! Right here in the ol' bag. Gonna cost ya!"

Feit grabbed the bag.

"Whoa there!" Chais said. "Finder's keepers."

"We have little time!" Feit said. "Tyran will be here any minute now."

"Who?"

Erich answered instead. "He's the one who killed the guards and prisoners."

Chais paused. "Well you'd better suit up," he said, handing him his bag. "I'll charge you later."

Erich pulled out the parts of his suit and Feit looked in the empty bag.

"You seem to have forgotten my attire!"

"Oh, that worthless tunic. I can't make money off of that."

"And what about my guns?"

Chais shrugged. "Beats me."

Erich attached parts to his legs, arms, chest, and back, and let the suit do the work. The mechanical pieces grew over his body and connected together, forming his Echelon armor.

"Now I believe you have some explaining to do, sir," Feit said to Erich. "You apparently have a history with this demented fellow."

Erich paused and lowered his head. "Aaron, well, Tyran, was a Xavacon Bounty Hunter whose obsession for power led to his downfall." He checked his armor systems to make sure they were functional. "He stole a substance being tested by my father meant for creatures called merics."

"Merics, you say?"

"Yes. The merics feed on energy from other life-forms, and we harvest the merics' powers to fuel our livelihood. The magnoplasm was meant to create energy for them so they can break their dependence on feeding on other living things. It wasn't meant for humans. But Tyran used it anyway. He has since been addicted to it."

"Didn't someone try to stop him?"

"Well, I battled him on planet Arcous, and he was banned from that star system."

"You fought him and let that monster live?" Feit asked.

"He's not a monster," Erich said, attaching his two armlets that contained his pulse wires. "The substance he injects in his body makes him go out of control. I need to find a way to help him—to extract the substance from his body."

"You're too kind, Erich. Too kind."

"He's here," Chais said, pointing.

Tyran passed by a few bystanders who stepped back in fear.

"So, you knew where to meet me," Tyran said. "Then you know why I'm here."

"I won't let you pass!" Feit said.

Tyran approached them with his head lowered and his eyes peering up. He stopped in front of Chais.

"Well now, did you bring them?" Tyran asked.

Chais nodded and removed two guns from his cloak. He handed them to Tyran.

"You traitorous theif!" Feit yelled but ran at Tyran instead to retrieve the weapons. Tyran shot at Feit's feet with the gravity gun but Feit leaped in the air. He came down with a punch to Tyran's face. Tyran tilted back from the hit but swiftly spun back around and punched him in the chest. Feit slid back and crumbled to his knees over the increased gravity spot Tyran created.

Erich shot a wire at Tyran, but Tyran dodged it. With his body leaning back, Tyran fired a gravity blast at Erich's feet, making him collapse.

"Tyran!" Erich yelled. He slowly stood back up with help from his suit but Tyran turned the dial up, increasing the gravity.

Erich collapsed to the surface again.

"It's futile," Tyran said. He approached Feit instead and slashed him in his shoulder with his claw.

Feit screamed in pain.

Chais unsheathed his sword. "What are you doing?!"

"Having a bit of fun!" Tyran said.

Chais looked at Feit and Erich who struggled to sit up. It reminded of the intense gravity on Earth. They could die from lack of blood flow to the brain. That's what Vecto had told him.

"All right. You got what you came for," Chais said. "Now you have to fulfill your side of the bargain."

Tyran cocked his head to the side.

"No. I have to torment Erich," Tyran said but stabbed Feit in the shoulder instead.

Feit grunted but took the pain.

"Stop—stop it!" Erich yelled despite the gravity constraining his speech.

"You see," Tyran said, "Erich hates killing. He hates death. His own body is irrelevant. What truly torments him is when he's helpless—unable to save another."

"No," Chais said, raising his sword, realizing what Tyran meant. "We had a deal!"

"The deal was for me to spare your friends' lives?" Tyran said. "But you're not his friend, are you?"

"You glockin' piece of trash!" Chais said as he slung his sword and detached the blade.

Tyran dodged the blade as it sliced through his hair, then fired at Chais. He wasn't there. He looked up to see Chais tossing a capsule. Tyran jumped to the side, grabbing the chain from Chais' Crossblade. The capsule exploded to release purple fibers but missed its target. Tyran yanked the chain to bring Chais toward him.

Chais let go of his sword, reached in his cloak and tossed ninja stars at him. But Tyran dodged them.

Still flying toward Tyran, Chais kicked him in the face.

Tyran fired the gravity gun and spun around, kicking Chais to the ground.

Chais fell in the gravity spot.

Tyran cocked his head and laughed. He looked at Erich, helpless on the floor, his body being crushed by the gravity, and clicked a button on the gravity gun to release Erich. Then Tyran formed a mask formed over his face and body and faded away from sight. "Their blood is yours, Erich," his voice said.

The green-and-black-looking planet shrank from view as Vecto rushed across the hull. It was a lot quicker travelling on the hull then through crowds in the ship—and less noticeable. Reentry would be a different story.

He didn't have time to reenter unnoticed. He would have to bust through a viewport and would surely be seen doing it. But at this point, he didn't care. He found a suitable window near the portside entry bay. Behind it was what he feared. Erich stood over an injured Feit, and nearby was Chais on the ground.

"You traitor!" Vecto yelled. He smashed his fist into the window. The metal-like glass cracked and Vecto punched it again.

He could see Feit screaming. He couldn't hear it in space, but he didn't have to.

Vecto punched harder and the window's crack grew.

Erich lifted his arm, pointing a weapon at Feit.

Vecto had to hurry. He only needed only one more punch.

Then the unspeakable happened. Erich shot him.

Vecto screamed and punched his fist through the glass. The window shattered. Air sucked out into space, and Vecto did a forward roll. He used his shield to block the airflow into space. An emergency door slammed shut behind to seal the breach.

As soon as it shut, Vecto jetted for Erich. In a flash, Vecto had Erich by the throat. He ran to the wall and slammed him against it.

Erich gasped. "Rob?"

"I am not Rob, you traitor," Vecto said. "I am Vecto!" Just when he was about to crush his neck, he felt pain against his back. He looked back to see white energy swirling around him.

"Vecto ..." Feit said, clutching a wire that Erich shot at him. "Run!"

Vecto then realized that Feit was in a gravity well and that Erich had shot a wire at Feit to free him if Vecto hadn't of stopped him.

Vecto's image of Robert Newman flickered off and on and he let go of Erich.

Energy swirled around him violently. He knew it was Leroy Johnson's energy, but where did it come from?

A laugh echoed across the room, followed by another shot. The gravity intensified around Vecto and Erich, causing Vecto to fall to his knees and Erich to land on his chest.

"Ah, Vecto, right?" Tyran said. "Right in the nick of time, eh?"

"What do you want with me?!" Vecto yelled, trying to resist the energy and gravity pull. He scanned the area to pinpoint his location, but the voice was coming from speakers. Any life signs were masked as well.

"I could care less about you," Tyran said. "It's Erich who I'm tormenting."

"Tyran!" Erich yelled. He no longer cared about the gravity. He no longer cared about his body. He pushed his body up and locked his knees underneath in an attempt to stand. He couldn't believe that Rob was really Vecto—his hero from when he was a child. All this must have been an illusion. A very sick one at that.

Vecto looked at Erich. "I'm sorry," Vecto said. "I was the fool to lie and doubt you."

"Ah, meaningless sentimental garbage spouted by the weak," Tyran said. He uncloaked himself in front of them with Feit's energy gun in his hand.

"What would happen if I fired another shot?" He inserted another energy cartridge into the gun. "Would it kill the mighty Vecto?"

"Stop it!" Erich yelled, still trying to get up. Erich lifted his body up straight, pushing himself from the floor.

"So ten times gravity isn't enough. How about twenty?" Tyran reached for his gravity gun, but it was missing.

"You forgot something," Chais said behind him. Before Tyran could turn, Chais stabbed him in the back with his sword. Tyran coughed up blood and looked back at Chais in shock.

"How did you—"

"I don't care!" Chais said. He yanked his blade out from his body.

Tyran closed his eyes and fell limp to the ground.

Using the gravity gun he stole back, Chais switched off the gravity. He couldn't help Vecto, though. Vecto's shields were nearly gone.

"About time, traitor," Feit said as he rolled over in relief, holding his shoulder.

"Had to wait for an opening, thank you very much," Chais said.

"Vecto?" Erich said as he touched his flickering body. He recoiled, looked at Tyran's body, and shook his head.

"His shields took quite the beating with that blast," Feit said, standing up.

"What kind of gun is that, anyway?" Chais asked. "Why didn't you tell me it can do that?"

"You had no business stealing it in the first place!" Feit scolded Chais. "And then giving it to the enemy of all people!"

Chais raised his sword. "I did what I could to save you two!"

"To save yourself is more accurate!"

"Guys, chill!" Erich yelled. "How do we save Vecto?"

"I am sorry," Vecto said, leaning over. "I have deceived myself. I cannot hold my shields much longer."

A familiar laughter echoed across the room.

They looked back at Tyran's body to see him rise as if zombie, his arms limp and head tilted down. His body glowed as his wound patched itself.

"Magnoplasm." Vecto recognized the energy. It was what Gyro was made of.

"The dead shall rise, and the weak, demised," Tyran said.

He swiftly lifted his arm and fired at Vecto.

Erich yelled Vecto's name and jumped in the way. The energy struck him in the chest, encompassing him.

Why, Vecto thought. Why would Erich try to save him? He barely knew Erich, and he even tried to kill him.

Erich stood in the midst of the energy. He glowed

white as his shoulder repaired itself. He wasn't hurt at all—just the opposite. Leroy's energy was healing him, just like it did for Leroy. Vecto remembered what Leroy had said. It hurts only opposing energy. It's hurting Vecto because of his hatred state of mind. But it was too late for him now. Vecto curled over and his image of Robert Newman shut off. It was followed by all three shields collapsing, exposing his orb. The ball of metal clanged against the surface and rolled.

Erich reached down to pick Vecto's orb up.

"I tried," he said.

"Ah, so it has the opposite effect on humans," Tyran said.

"I won't let you have him!" Erich said as he clutched the orb.

"Oh, you can keep it," Tyran said. "My prize is your suffering."

Erich walked over to Feit and touched him on the shoulder. Erich was still glowing and healed his wound. He then handed him Vecto's orb to take care of. With no shields, Vecto couldn't talk. He couldn't move. He was limited, and Erich figured Feit knew best how to handle him.

Erich got into fighting stance, followed by Chais and Feit. "I'm ready when you are."

Tyran laughed and walked around them. "Not yet, dear children." He stopped in front of a massive bay door.

"It's time for the encore!" Tyran lifted his palms in the air. "Rise!"

In obedience, the massive bay door behind him jolted and slowly rose. Its shadow moved farther from the bay door as it lifted, scrolling up the bodies of robots—rows of them, hundreds of them.

"Come forth!" Tyran ordered.

The robots' eyes lit up red and they obeyed Tyran, marching forward.

Chais exercised his wrist. "We had a deal!"

Tyran raised his hand to stop the robots just behind him. "I freed you from jail. I didn't kill you. Isn't that enough?"

"I got you your stupid weapon and still went back to jail for your murders!"

"Well ..." Tyran said. He moved red hair from his face. "In that case: Robots, kill everyone except them!"

The army of robots marched by Tyran, swallowing him in the crowd.

Tyran smirked, a red dot within the metallic walking mass. "And Sarah—sound the evacuation alarms."

11

"Wait, me buccaneer! Where ye headed?" Cutlass asked as he ran after Trip. He stopped amid the crowd and leaned over to take a breath, then rubbed his forehead. He had a headache from the alarms, and he was losing sight of Trip in the crowd. It would have been easier if Trip were going in the same direction as the evacuees.

"I-I've got to find Erich!" Trip yelled back. "He's locked up. H-he's going to be stuck here if I don't do anything!"

Cutlass could barely hear him from all of the panic-induced screaming around him—plus the alarms, but he heard Erich's name and wasn't going to let Trip go alone.

"Great! They're avoiding us!" Feit said with sarcasm as he ran after a robot.

"They're going after the civilians!" Erich yelled, shooting pulse wires to grab a few robots and slinging them back. The glow from his body had already faded.

Feit grabbed one of these flying robots with his free hand and slung it to the side so the wire attached would trip up others. People rushed down the halls, screaming, as the machines rapidly fired at them.

"It doesn't help that all the doors were opened for evacuation. It's putting everyone right in their paths!" Feit jumped on a running robot and smashed Vecto's orb into its head. "Sorry, Vecto!"

Erich dragged the two robots from before behind him, and yanked the wires, slinging them around to knock into other machines.

"A gun would help!" Feit said as he ducked one of the wires passing overhead. He then grabbed a robot's arm and yanked it as it fired. He tackled it to the floor and pointed the gun arm at another robot, letting the bullets destroy it.

As he ran, Erich detached what was left of the machines from the wires and lit up the cords with pulse energy. Energy buzzed through the wires as they streaked a burn trail behind. He swung the loose wires around, slashing robots in half, then snapped the energy cords like a whip, cracking holes in their chests.

Feit turned his attention to him, impressed. But priorities came first. "All right, sir, listen up. We can't forget about Tyran. He's using these machines as a diversion for him to escape." Feit slung a robot at Erich and a wire slashed through it. "Can you take him out?"

"With my suit, of course," Erich said as he chased down another machine and slashed its head off. "But we've got to protect the civilians first!"

"There won't be anything left if Tyran gets away!" Feit said as he grabbed the severed head in midair and threw it at a robot before it shot down another civilian. "What if he intends to blow up the ship? Then we're all lost!" He flipped over another robot and grabbed its head, then tossed it over him as he landed. "Look, I'll take care of things here. You seem to have a history with Tyran, so I assume you're the best bet to handle him."

Erich jumped over dead bodies sprawled against the floor and slid to a stop. He couldn't save them. The robots were faster. But if he could beat Tyran, he could prevent more deaths. Feit was right.

"Chais is covering the other hall. Now go!" Erich heard Feit's trailing voice. He saw Feit pick up loose items on the floor as he ran and tossed them at machines in the distance.

Erich spun around and headed the opposite direction. The most likely place Tyran would run off to would be the ship's docking bay, he thought. He only hoped he was right.

When Feit looked back, a missile was heading for a civilian. Feit spun up, still clutching the robot's arm, and slung the machine in the missile's path. The two exploded, and Feit continued his hunt. But it surprised him when one of the robots fired a missile at the ceiling instead of a person. Feit quickly understood why. The roof collapsed, and bodies from the upper floor fell with the rubble. The robots leaped through the opening to kill more, and Feit followed. He couldn't save everyone—he knew that much. But for every robot he destroyed, that meant dozens of lives saved.

"Mommy, I'm scared!" a little girl said, weeping.

"Shh! We've got to be quite," her mother whispered.

It was dark, and the stench of sweat was unbearable in the crowded storage room, but they were safe from the robots here. If they sprinted for the escape pods on the far side of the ship, who's to say there would be any pods left, and who's to say they would even survive?

There was a bang at the door and the little girl held tight to her mom. There was another bang in front of where they crouched. A stream of light shone through the newly-made crack in the door. Metallic fingers shot through the crack, and the girl screamed, followed by cries throughout the room.

The robot yanked the two elevator-style doors open a few inches and peered inside. The mother muffled her daughter's mouth and wrapped her in her arms for protection. She closed her eyes.

The occupants heard a metal clash and grinding, but they were still alive. The mother opened her eyes to see a sword sticking out from the robot, straight through the opening in the door. The robot was cut nearly in half, from the top down.

"Stupid blade," Chais said, yanking the robot's body back with his sword in it. "I gotta sharpen this thing," he mumbled to himself as he kicked the robot from his blade. "Y'all OK?" he asked, peering in. "I can escort you to the pods."

"Thank you, thank you," the mother said as tears rolled down her cheeks. "But will we make it?"

"Don't worry—as long as you stay near me, they won't fire. Long story."

The mother gasped as she saw through the crack several robots approaching.

The robots raised their guns but didn't fire. Chais stood in front of their targets.

"Yeah, that's right! You can't kill me and the others—master's orders." Chais retracted his sword and hooked it to his side, then swung open his trench coat and pulled out two automatic handguns with extended clips. "This will be interesting!" he said as he opened fire.

It was pitch-black in the docking bay when Erich entered. Quiet, too. But Erich knew Tyran was here.

"Show yourself!" Erich yelled.

"Sarah—lights, please," Tyran's voice echoed back.

The docking bay lit to reveal a vast array of spacecraft parked to the left, stretching down the rear of the ship. The canopies were eye level, bridged with panel connectors. They were on the second floor with offices to the right used to monitor traffic. Erich searched for Tyran and looked up to see him leaning against the rail of a catwalk. Tyran's long, red hair spewed over the rail, covering his face.

"So you abandoned your friends to fight me—abandoned all those civilians you could have saved," Tyran said with a smirk seen through strands of his hair.

"I'm saving more by facing you!" Erich cut back. Impulsively, he shot a wire at him. The air caused the tip of the wire to split into three and they grabbed Tyran's face, hair and all.

Tyran stumbled, and Erich yanked the wire, pulling Tyran's head forward, tossing him over the catwalk. Tyran circled around and landed on his feet. He was crouched over, head down. But he was laughing.

"Look at me!" Erich said, tugging the wire to make Tyran look up. He dislodged the wire from his face, reeling the cord back in his armlet. Then he noticed two swords in Tyran's hand, their blades stretched outward.

Tyran's hair rolled across his face as he lifted his head and rose. He flipped the handle of one of the swords to face Erich. It was Erich's sword. Its blade was shaped like red and white flames, attached to a hilt of the same colors.

"You messed up my face," Tyran said sardonically. "Here, use this. It'll leave a larger mark."

Erich stared at the blade in disbelief. It was his old sword.

"You miss this, don't you?" Tyran said. "You could have killed me with this. Why not try again?" Tyran motioned Erich to take it.

Memories flashed in Erich's mind of the last time he used it; it was against Tyran a few months ago. He spared Tyran's life and abandoned the sword.

Erich found his hand edging closer to it but pulled back.

Tyran noticed Erich's reluctance and tossed the sword at him. Erich snatched its handle on reflex, then Tyran raised his nearly identical sword, its blade and handle covered in black and red.

"Go ahead, Erich. Take your revenge," Tyran taunted. "Think of all those innocent people I've killed on this ship. Think of the misery I've caused you."

Erich lifted the sword and looked at its blade—still sharp—still shinny. He could use it once more—to take revenge. But something about the blade caught his eyes. He could see his reflection and it reminded him of his promise to never use it again.

Erich lowered the weapon, shaking his head.

"No," he said. "Our weapons were made for death. I can't go down the path you took. Look at you. It only leads to self-destruction."

Tyran frowned.

Erich tossed it aside, tuning out the clang it made against the hard floor. "I no longer need it," he said.

"You're going down without it!"

Erich lunged at Tyran and swung his fist. Tyran dodged to the left and came down with his sword. Erich turned back and blocked the blade with the cover for his pulse wire armlet, knocking the blade away. Now with an opening, Erich circled that same arm into a gut punch. He then shot a pulse wire into Tyran's chest.

Tyran stumbled back from the force and looked at his stomach. It wasn't a piercing tip, but it was attached to his suit.

"You forgot to make it sharp," Tyran said and laughed. He grabbed the wire and yanked it to throw Erich, but Erich didn't budge. He was only pulling more wire out.

"So you think those pathetic wires of yours can do the trick?" Tyran said. "Are you going to capture me? Put me in jail? Then what? I'll just escape!" Tyran let go of the wire and swung his blade at Erich.

"I won't let you!" Erich yelled, blocking it with his armlet shield, then again and again.

When Tyran pulled back, his sword resisted. Erich had grabbed the slack from the wire and wrapped it around Tyran's blade. Erich flipped over Tyran and swirled the wire around his neck as he passed overhead. He landed, locked the wire in place and yanked it until the Tyran's wrapped sword rested against his throat.

"Give up, Tyran," Erich said. "I can send energy through this wire and slice your head off."

"Mm. Morbid. But you won't kill me," Tyran said and laughed.

Erich tugged on the wire and Tyran turned around with the sword's blade still tied to his neck. He let go of the sword, letting it inch closer to his neck.

"Look, we don't have to do this," Erich said. "You can call off the robots, and I'll let you live."

"Let me?" Tyran questioned. "You are in no position to make commands." He walked toward him.

"Have you gone psycho since I left?" Erich said. "I can still kill you."

"You won't," Tyran said and reached out his arms as if he wanted a hug.

"Don't test me!" Erich said and tugged the wire.

Tyran stopped only a few feet from Erich, his arms still stretched forward.

"You see, you hate killing," Tyran said. "But I, on the other hand, don't abide by the same morals."

"I could care less if I died!" Erich said, tugging the wires again, this time causing blood to trickle down Tyran's neck.

Tyran resisted the choking sensation, ignoring the sword tied to his neck.

"Oh, not you," he said. "Trip and Cutlass!"

Tyran grabbed the wires and yanked them forward. Erich still had them locked and was thrown toward him. Tyran punched him in the gut, and when Erich bowed forward, Tyran wrapped the slack of wires around Erich's neck, too, and yanked the wire to choke him.

Erich jerked upward and went for a breath but couldn't. He detached the wires from his gun and freed himself, stumbling back while coughing.

Tyran then unwrapped the wires from around his neck and pulled his sword loose.

"Leave them out of this!" Erich managed to cough out.

"It's too late for that," Tyran said. "Sarah!"

A holographic image appeared against the wall to Erich's right. It appeared across the room, in the air. It popped up everywhere. The screens displayed a live feed from the ship's surveillance videos. It showed Trip and Cutlass.

* * *

It was awkwardly silent in the hall Trip stood in. The evacuees were long gone from this point, but bodies remained.

"W-why do so many people have to die?' Trip asked as he kneeled down.

"It be important to save 'em, then, eh?" Cutlass said and laid a hand on Trip's shoulder.

"Th-they're dead, you imbecile!"

"There be some mateys on this ship yet to be shark bait, me boy. It'd be me pleasure to save me crew!"

"Forget it!" Trip yelled, reaching for his handkerchief to wipe his eyes. "W-what can we do? N-n-nothing!"

"We can save Erich, me buccaneer."

Trip shook his head. "I-I … I don't think—"

The ceiling nearby exploded and a dozen robots fell with the rubble. Trip looked up and heard the sound of machine gun discharge.

"Trip!" Cutlass yelled.

Bullets struck Trip in the chest.

"You …" Erich said, trying to discredit the video, trying to believe it was just fake. "You're beyond sadistic!"

"You like that, don't you?" Tyran said, watching the video play across the hanger bay.

Erich looked down, trying to avoid the video, trying to avoid the pain. But even the floor showed the scene.

Cutlass snatched a shield capsule from his sleeve and threw it at Trip. The capsule smashed into his back.

Trip's body jolted violently after each shot until a shield formed around him and Cutlass.

"Trip! Trip!" Cutlass yelled as he grabbed Trip with his

one arm as the kid collapsed. The robots kept firing at the shields, unloading ammunition and missiles, but the shield held for the moment.

"Trip! Say something!"

Trip attempted a smile as he lifted his head. "Y-you idiot! Y-your voice. It's normal. ... Y-your memory? Is it back?"

"Arrgh! Don't move, me lad! Ye don't need to feed the fish!"

Nope, Cutlass is the same, Trip thought. He laughed until it turned into a cough, trying to think about something else than the bullets in his body.

"Me buccaneer ... me buccaneer! Don't ye give in, lad!" Cutlass laid him on the floor to rest. More robots dropped from the ceiling until there were dozens beating the temporary shield.

"Don't forget me," he said to Trip.

What's he talking about? Trip saw a tear roll down Cutlass' cheek and understood. "W-wait! ... Yo-you're not—"

Cutlass yelled a war cry and slammed his fist into the surface. The floor caved in below them and a shockwave of energy rippled across the room, knocking the robots off their feet. "You scurvy, yellow-bellied sapsucker, bilge rat, gasbags!!" Cutlass yelled, raising his fist in the air.

Trip kept blinking, wondering if he was seeing things. Flame devoured Cutlass' arm as he forced the arm to bend the other way. In the most disgusting thing Trip had ever seen, he watched Cutlass' arm crack the other direction and skin and blood splatter from the reversed joint. But most unbelievable of all was that Cutlass' sole arm was cybernetic underneath the skin. That's all Trip remembered before his eyes closed.

The shield flickered and Cutlass ran out from it.

"I'll keel haul ye mangy cockroaches!" Cutlass yelled and fired a rapid slew of energy beams from his deformed elbow. He destroyed several as he ran at them. Then he fired missiles from the compartment of his forearm to destroy others as he jumped in the air and fired down on them, landing on one particularly battered robot. A bullet pierced his back, then his leg, and Cutlass fell to one knee, but he continued to unleash streams of bullets and trails of missile smoke. He took down as many as he could until his gun arm overheated. His elbow smoked as he lowered it. There were still ten robots left. Then twelve … and fourteen. More robots fell from the ceiling until dozens remained once again. They marched around to flank him.

Cutlass looked over at Trip within the weakened shield—he was lifeless—then he stared back at the leftover machines that encircled him. He ripped off his eye patch and tossed it aside—it revealed a mechanical eye. Cutlass bent his deformed arm back in place and struck his fingers in his right eye socket. He yanked the false eye out and raised his arm triumphantly, holding it in the air. "Dead men tell no tales!"

The robots fired, and bullets pierced Cutlass' body, some exiting him, but Cutlass's hand with the eyeball was already headed fast for the metallic floor. He smashed the eye bomb against the surface, causing it to explode. A burst of flame and energy jettisoned from it, ripping the metal bodies surrounding him, sending scrap metal down the halls. The floor and ceiling collapsed, and the walls bulged.

When the explosion settled, Trip's body was still in the shield as mechanical parts showered around him. There were no more robots.

And there was no more Cutlass.

* * *

"Noo!!" Erich yelled after watching the video.

"You are helpless," Tyran said. "Don't you realize?"

"If this is how you want to be," Erich said with his head low, letting a wire from each arm uncoil from his gun. "Then I have no choice."

"What? Are you going to whip me?" Tyran quipped.

The wires touched the ground as they extended, but they started to glow. Pulse energy coursed through the wires as he walked toward Tyran. The wires dragged with him, burning trails in the metal surface.

"Ah, that's more like it," Tyran said with a smirk. "I await your agony!"

Erich yelled and ran toward Tyran. He slashed at him with the deadly energy but Tyran jumped back. Erich sliced a pole in the way and followed as Tyran leaped from one spacecraft to the next. He missed Tyran again and slashed the nose off a ship with his energized whip. He looked around searching for him. He saw him standing on a catwalk.

"I've grown much stronger than when you banished me from bounty school," Tyran said.

"I only see a coward."

"Speed is a form of power, Erich."

Erich activated his boosters and came at Tyran.

"I've had to live the life of a pirate since then!" Tyran yelled as he jumped off the catwalk. "Do you even understand the pain you caused?"

Erich sliced the catwalk in half and flew through the two parts. "What are you talking about? What about the pain *you* caused? You killed my friends. You deserted us!"

Tyran landed. "And you murdered my soul! Why are you the chosen one? Why not me?" He jumped back to avoid the whip as Erich landed before him. "I was the top of the class. I was the best fighter. Yet you were the favored one!"

Tyran raised his arm and fired explosive shells at Erich.

Erich ran toward the wall, avoiding the blasts. "I didn't choose that path! It was forced upon me! I left the Golen Station for that reason!"

"You left to torture me!"

"I left because I couldn't kill!" Erich dropped the energy from his whip and shot a wire at his sword's hilt on the ground. He used the wall to propel himself forward toward Tyran.

"You made me, Erich!" Tyran said as he unsheathed his sword and jumped toward him.

Erich swung the blade attached to the wire. It came at Tyran, but he blocked it and spun around in the air. He had the opening and struck Erich on the top of his shoulder. They both crashed to the surface. Erich dropped to his knees while Tyran dug the blade in deeper.

"It's over," Tyran said. "You have beaten me before. Never again!"

Erich grabbed Tyran's hilt and pushed the blade out of him.

"You'll never win!"

Tyran kneed Erich in the face, threw the blade aside and stabbed Erich in the other shoulder with his claw.

"You cannot win this time!" He dragged Erich to a nearby console and punched him in the face.

Erich's vision blurred as he yanked the wire with the attached sword toward him. Tyran knocked the blade way. He grabbed Erich by the head and smashed his skull in the console. Again and again he smashed it until Erich went unconscious.

Tyran let go of him and stood over his body. He reached to his side to remove a syringe. "You will mirror my fate," he said.

Chais opened the docking bay doors to see Tyran leaning over Erich with a needle.

I'm too late, he thought.

"Oh, have you come to see the fight?" Tyran said as he stood. "Come again tomorrow."

"What did you do to him?" Chais yelled.

"Nothing that matters to you."

"Leave him to me," a robot said to Chais. "Save Erich."

A clunky robot with an orb in its chest stepped out from behind Chais. It was Vecto within Azmeck's robot.

"You've managed to obtain a rusty body, I see," Tyran said, "with a lack of shields."

"You're wrong." Vecto took deliberately slow steps toward Tyran as a force field flickered over his body.

"Ah, those pesky shields. Just wait—you'll kneel before me!" Tyran pulled out the energy gun and fired a capsule at Vecto. Vecto kept walking. Leroy's energy didn't even faze him this time.

Tyran inserted the last shell, a bit hesitant. "Very well, I will become you!" He fired at himself.

Tyran fell to one knee in pain. The energy burned him, draining his power. He expected the energy to boost his power as it did Erich, but it had the opposite effect.

Tyran looked at his shriveled hand. "How?"

"The energy only hurts the evil in one's self," Vecto said. "I'm not going to be like you. I've done that. There's only misery and defeat." He dropped his shield to show Tyran he didn't need them.

"Another Erich, you fool!" Tyran punched with his clawed arm.

Vecto reached his hand out and let the claw pierce through his palm. The blade stuck out from the back of his metal hand as Vecto twisted his wrist and snapped the blade in half.

"I am a machine that chooses his own destiny!" Vecto reactivated his shields and grabbed Tyran by the arm, burning them.

Tyran pulled out a syringe, but it was empty. Vecto grabbed it and crushed it.

"Sarah!" Tyran yelled. "Open the bay doors!"

Vecto was startled hearing her name. The bay doors opened, gushing wind in the room. The ship never left Hodos' orbit. It was reentering the atmosphere, possibly to let Tyran escape to the surface.

"Don't worry," Chais said. "I've got Erich." He held him with one arm as he held onto his sword in the other. Its blade and chain were wrapped around the console.

"What did you do to Sarah?!" Vecto demanded.

"Let go, and I'll tell," Tyran said, looking up through strands of his hair.

"Don't do it!" Chais said.

"As well as Zendora's location."

"How did you—?"

"I know lots about you, Vecto," Tyran said and smirked.

Vecto released his grip on Tyran, and he stood. The magnoplasm in his body was already healing the damage done from the self-inflicted blast.

"Vecto! He's bluffing!" Chase said. "He could easily have learned that you're seeking Zendora!"

Vecto ignored Chais. "You learned this from Sarah, I

assume. What did you do to her?"

"No, Vecto. I learned this from Morphaal!"

Tyran laughed and leaped up. He landed on what seemed to be air. The air beneath him flickered and revealed a cockpit and mech that was previously cloaked. Tyran was swallowed by his Turmoil mech before Vecto could react.

"No!" Vecto smashed his fist into the console. "Not Morphaal!"

The Turmoil leaped back and fell outside the docking bay.

"He's getting away!" Chais yelled, his hair flapping forward as he held onto the console.

Vecto looked at Chais and was reminded of him running after Chais when they first met.

"You of all people know he can't escape," Vecto said. He ran and jumped out the open bay doors.

Tyran's Turmoil mech fell toward planet Hodos, its hull burning from atmospheric entry. The mech looked back to see the ship shrinking in the distance in front of a backdrop of stars. Tyran then saw a flaming object pierce the air like a bullet, descending toward his mech.

"Persistent, eh?" Tyran turned the mech's back to the flames and shot at the object. It swerved to dodge and slammed into the Turmoil's chest. The mech picked Vecto off it and tossed him aside. It activated boosters and jetted back toward the ship. Vecto used his shield to suck the air around him, then condensed it under him and burst it below to give him a boost.

The Turmoil looked back to see Vecto coming after it. Tyran fired missiles down at him, but Vecto dodged them. He grabbed a missile and slung it back.

The Turmoil mech shielded itself with its arm as Vecto slammed a fist into the mech's chest. The mech grabbed Vecto again and spun around as it approached the Corona. It threw Vecto into the hull of the ship. The mech landed on its flaming belly and jetted beneath it.

"Sarah, take the ship back into space!" Tyran yelled.

The nose turned upward and the ship slowed. The Turmoil headed for the other side. It landed on the top hull as the ship changed directions and began to ascend. Tyran waited. The ship exited the atmosphere and Tyran sighed in relief. Tyran knew that Vecto couldn't fight in space. His shields can't breathe. He had only a moment's rest when he saw Vecto shoot out from the ship's exterior. Pieces of the ship scattered out from the pierced hull as Vecto flexed his shields and catapulted the pieces at the mech. The Turmoil blocked the pieces with a swing of the arm and ignited an energy blade.

Vecto hovered over the ship with air blasting from beneath him, his bulky body deteriorating in his shields.

"If you kill me, you'll never find Zendora," Tyran said through his mech's speakers.

"Even if you knew, you'd lie to me," Vecto said. "You have nothing to bargain with but bluffs."

"Oh contraire!" Tyran yelled. "I have Sarah!" The mech came at Vecto with its energy sword, but Vecto dodged it.

The Turmoil jumped back. "Destroy him, Sarah!"

Vecto came at the mech but gun turrets surfaced from the hull and fired.

The Turmoil jetted in space as the guns fired at Vecto.

Vecto spun to dodge and jetted after him.

The Turmoil fired down at Vecto. *I have to stall Vecto*, Tyran thought. He had to suffocate his shields from carbon.

The mech and robot clashed as the ship rose to meet them. They landed back on the ship and exchanged swings as energy beams struck them. Vecto slid to a stop and yanked a turret from the ship, directing its fire at the mech. The Turmoil slashed the beams with its sword and cut a piece out from the hull. It kicked the piece up to use it as a shield. Pieces began to float away in space.

"You've lost!" Tyran yelled, although Vecto couldn't hear him. He directed the mech to charge at him with the makeshift shield in one hand and a sword in the other.

Vecto let it come. He let the blade strike his shields, then he punched the mech's metal shield, expanding his force field into the shape of a blade, piercing through the metal barrier and through the mech.

The Turmoil landed on its knee. Vecto sliced the shield in half and swung his arm around. He stabbed the mech in the shoulder with his edged force field shield.

Vecto grabbed the cockpit and ripped the frame off. He stared inside to see an empty cockpit. It was operated by remote. Tyran escaped after all.

12

Hours later, Vecto stood in Azmeck's lab as Azmeck worked on Trip and Erich. He was flanked by Feit and Chais.

"Will they be all right?" Chais asked.

Azmeck looked at Chais and lowered his goggles. "As for Trip, he has some extraordinary healing abilities and will be OK. I cannot say the same for Erich. He keeps slipping in and out of consciousness. His body seems to be fighting with his mind, which is deteriorating."

Trip mumbled in his sleep. "Th-that idiot!" He rolled over. "Why'd y-you do it, Cutlass!"

"Be calm," Feit said at his side.

Vecto walked toward Erich, his clunky deteriorated body screeching with each step. "It's my fault," he said. "I should have been there sooner."

"It's not your doing, sir," Feit said. "You went as fast as you could after I gave you that body."

Vecto nodded and the door opened. Accura stepped through.

"How's the guard duty?" Chais asked.

"I eliminated several robots, so I subdued them for now," Accura said, resting a rifle on her shoulder. "They're not looking for a fight, anyway. They're more interested in making sure everyone is contained and doesn't escape."

"Any word on Tyran?" Feit asked.

"Not a peep," Accura said. "What does he want?"

"He got what he wants," Feit said. "For Erich to suffer."

"I won't let him have that satisfaction," Vecto said. He knelt beside Erich's rest capsule. "Of all people, Erich does not deserve this. He had attempted to save my life, even after I tried to kill him. He jumped in front of that energy blast, unconcerned that it could have killed him. This selflessness is what I lost from my former self. It's what Gyro had shown but I have forgotten. If only there is a way for me to tell him this. To thank him for showing me the errors of my ways."

Vecto lowered his head.

"I could conceivably connect your minds," Azmeck said.

Vecto looked up as the others looked on.

"Remember that the purpose of this voyage was for me to find a way to connect into yours," Azmeck said.

"Whoa," Chais said. "You can do that?"

"Did you get it working already?" Feit asked.

"I had the machine on this ship," Azmeck explained. "It only needed some reprogramming."

Accura opened the door and peeked out for a moment to watch for robots.

Vecto slowly stood. "With this process, could I save his mind from deterioration?"

"I'm not quite sure to tell the truth," Azmeck said.

"You'll have to find its root cause. And if Erich dies in the process, there's no telling if you'll come back."

"Begin the procedure," Vecto said.

"Are you sure?" Azmeck asked a bit cautiously. "It hasn't been tested."

"I'm confident."

"Very well," Azmeck said. "I'll have to connect your orb to this." Azmeck pulled out what looked like a suction tube.

"Bring him back," Feit said.

"And don't die on me!" Chais said. "We have a deal, remember?"

Accura shook her head.

Vecto hovered his orb from the body. "Look after each other," Vecto said, attaching to the device.

He could feel the flow of thoughts. They swirled around him as if he stood in its center. There was joy, there was trust, there was anticipation, surprise, calmness, friendship; there was courage, confidence, kindness, and love. It was bliss to Vecto, real feelings, yet he had experienced them after all. He had long since felt these emotions. But in the midst of the glorified thoughts was an all-too familiar emotion: sadness.

"Erich," Vecto said. "Can you hear me?"

He felt his mind swirl into the sadness. He saw death, bullying, rejection, disappointment.

"Erich," Vecto said. "Speak to me. I want to thank you for saving me. You saved my mind. Let me save yours."

"Rob?" Erich's voice asked.

"Rob was a lie," Vecto said. "I'm sorry."

"I tried to kill him," Erich said. "I vowed not to, yet tried to."

"You mean Tyran?"

"He can be saved."

"But he's demented!"

"Weren't you?" Erich's voice began to fade.

Vecto searched his thoughts to see where he went.

"Promise me," Erich said, "promise me you won't kill anyone. Life is too valuable for that."

Vecto found him drifting into kindness.

"I can't guarantee you that," Vecto said.

Trust and a bit of joy swirled around Vecto. "Least you're honest," Erich said. "You'd better leave before it takes over."

"What do you mean?" Vecto asked.

Vecto moved his mind around and felt darkness descend on them.

"What is that?"

"It is what enslaves Tyran," Erich said. "And it will enslave me."

"Magnoplasm," Vecto thought.

"Yes."

"I can control it," Vecto said. If Gyro could control it, so could he.

"You must leave."

"Trust me."

"Something's wrong," Azmeck said. "He's losing a pulse!"

Erich's body jolted, convulsing.

"Shut it off!" Chais said.

"If I do, there's no return!"

"We can't just sit here and do nothing!" Feit said.

"L-let me try," a voice said.

"Trip?" Azmeck said. "You are in no condition to—"

Trip slipped his feet into his shoes and walked over

to Erich.

"I-I know why Cutlass pro-protected me," Trip said. He reached out and touched Erich—with nothing. Yet energy coursed from his hand into Erich.

"I c-can reject germs, re-reject foreign objects, reject a-anything I want," Trip said. "I-if it wasn't for C-Cutlass, I w-would be indefinitely immured for testing."

"Vecto," a voice said.

"Sarah?" Vecto asked. "What are you doing here? What happened to you?"

"You must escape, Vecto," Sarah's voice said. "There's a mighty virus Tyran is using against me. No matter how many times I rewrite my code to free myself, it keeps undoing it. I cannot withstand its control much longer. If you stay here, the bridge to return will be broken."

"I have to save Erich," Vecto said. He thought about asking Sarah about the hundreds-of-years-old distress signal Acaterra received concerning Zendora, but now wasn't the time. Erich was more important.

"I have been ordered to sever the link," Sarah said. "You will be trapped here if you don't leave."

Vecto fought against the dark thoughts that swarmed around him. "It is nice to hear from you again, Sarah. I will have to take my chances."

"No!" Sarah said.

"You will be next. I promise."

"The machine's losing control!" Azmeck said, frantically searching for the issue.

"Shut it off!" Chais said.

"I can't!" Azmeck yelled. "It has a mind of its own!"

"If you don't, it'll kill them both!"

Azmeck shut off its power supply and wiped sweat from his forehead. The machine powered down but immediately rebooted with intensity. It was feeding off the power from Vecto's orb.

"Oh my! It's no good!" Azmeck said.

Accura raised her rifle and aimed her scope.

"It has been a pleasure, Vecto," she said.

The others looked back at her as she fired at the terminal.

It smoked from the blast and abruptly shut off. Vecto's orb rolled away from the suction tube and dropped from the table.

They stood in silence as it clanged on the floor—no shields, no life.

Accura walked to the orb and picked it up.

Azmeck lowered his head. "Vecto …"

"Don't think you'll get that bounty on him!" Chais said.

Accura handed Azmeck the orb. "See what you can do."

Azmeck nodded as Accura walked off. She slung her rifle over her shoulder and left the room.

"How's Erich?" Feit asked Trip.

"H-he's still alive," Trip said. "St-still unconscious."

"What do we do now?" Chais asked.

"Have faith," Feit responded.

Three days later, Erich stayed in a coma and Vecto's orb was unresponsive.

Feit, Accura, Chais, Trip, and Azmeck sat at a table discussing their options.

The gang had eliminated the robots, but they were still imprisoned. The ship was their prison. They couldn't take command of it, and whoever tried to flee in an escape pod was immediately shot down. Only Cutlass' escape pod that served as a casket made it out. And that was only because there were no life signs aboard. The group only hoped the distress signal on the pod would reach someone.

"Nothing on the distress signal yet," Feit said.

"Where in space are we, anyway?" Accura asked.

"I dunno," Chais said.

"Of course you don't!" Accura snapped back.

"Hey! It's not my fault I was sheltered on Zendora!"

"Would you please quit the bickering for once," Feit said and buried his head into his hand.

"We must find Tyran," Azmeck said.

"We t-t-tried!" Trip said.

"Then we'll try again tomorrow," Feit said. "We'll reconvene tomorrow at the same time." He stood up from the head of the table. "Get some sleep, everyone."

Erich awoke to the sounds of a video feed. He blinked and turned his head to the noise.

"Dr. Azmeck," he said.

Azmeck was lounged in a chair when he heard Erich's voice. He quickly spewed his drink and rushed over.

"You're alive!" Azmeck said.

Erich blinked. "Where am I?"

"You're in my lab. You had a terrible concussion."

"Dr. Azmeck," Erich said. He lifted one of his hands. "I have arms."

"Yes, indeed. You are quite intact."

Erich felt his face. He pinched himself to make sure he wasn't dreaming.

"I have feelings," he said.

"Are you OK?"

Erich sat up. "Where's my orb?"

"You're orb?" Azmeck questioned. "You mean Vecto?"

"Am I not Vecto?" Erich asked.

Azmeck gasped. "My word! Is it you, Vecto?"

"I seem to have acquired Erich's body," Vecto said as he stood up. "Have I failed to save him?"

Vecto wobbled on his feet and fell. Azmeck rushed to his aid.

"Be careful," Azmeck warned, lifting him up. "You're not used to it."

"Where's my orb?" Vecto asked again.

Azmeck laid him back on the rest capsule.

"No worries," Azmeck said. "It's over here." Azmeck shuffled to a container and opened it. But it was empty.

"Oh, no. Oh, no," Azmeck said. "It was just here last night!"

"Tyran came last night," Vecto said.

Azmeck arched an eyebrow. "And what makes you think that?"

"He spoke to me, but I was unable to move or talk back."

"Oh my!"

"I need Erich's suit," Vecto demanded. Vecto stood up again and struggled to walk. He grabbed onto a piece of machinery to brace himself.

"Now, now, Vecto," Azmeck said. "You must take it easy. You are in no condition to look for Tyran."

Vecto reached into the box and pulled out the red and white suit pieces.

"I know where he went," Vecto said, attaching the parts to his body. "He's waiting for me."

"You can't go like this!" Azmeck said. "You can barely walk! Let alone fight him. Tell the others where he's hiding."

"I will be OK," Vecto said, letting the suit automatically extend and attach together. "This is something I must do alone."

Vecto wobbled to the door and opened it.

"Vecto! Don't be so independent!" Azmeck said. "Learn from your mistakes, my lad. Use some teamwork for a change."

Vecto looked back. "Don't follow me, and don't try to stop me." He closed the door.

Vecto took slow steps across a metal grating catwalk. On each side were towering pillars of tubes filled with blue energy. Below him was a gray hazy pit of steam with no bottom in sight. He was in the engine room of the Corona, and in front of him, at the end of the catwalk, was the core, where Sarah's mainframe was held—where Tyran stood.

Tyran entered data in the console but stopped and peered through the fog. He smirked upon seeing Vecto.

"So you came alone after all," Tyran said. "How do you feel?"

Vecto ignored him, slowly making his approach, trying to contain his anger. The disk on his the back of his Eschalon suit spun and glowed yellow, fixed by Azmeck.

"Come, now, Erich," Tyran said. "I'm truly concerned. Vecto's attempt at freeing your mind could have destroyed you. If I didn't sever the link, you would have died."

"You liar!" Vecto said.

"Tell, me, why have you come?" Tyran asked. He twirled Vecto's orb in his hand. "Have you come for this? To save Vecto? Or do you still think I can be saved?"

"You killed Erich!" Vecto said. He stumbled to a stop and raised his armlet.

"Erich?" Tyran said. He walked through a gust of steam with a puzzled look on his face. "What have you done to Erich?!" He looked at Vecto's orb and then at Erich's body.

"I could have saved him!" Vecto said.

"You—you killed him, didn't you?!" Tyran yelled. "You snatched his body!" Tyran looked down, his head twitching. He took a syringe from his side and stabbed himself in the neck with it. His veins showed, turning red. Energy flowed around him, blowing his hair. He looked up with bloodshot eyes.

"Have you come to murder me?" Tyran asked.

"You're demented, Tyran!" Vecto said. "I couldn't save Erich, so I'm here to save Sarah!"

"No, no. Sarah is mine alone!" Tyran yelled, raising his explosion shell armlet gun at Vecto, peering over the bulky gun mounted on his arm.

"Give me back my orb, Tyran," Vecto said. "I can help you."

"Help me?" Tyran said and laughed. "You're not Erich. You can't help me!"

Vecto lowered his pulsewire armlet. "I know why you want Sarah. You want companionship—someone to talk to—someone you can control. But it doesn't have to be this way."

"You don't understand!" Tyran said.

"I understand that you kept Erich alive because he was the only one who cared about you. Yet you took joy out of torturing him because he shared your pain."

"You know nothing!"

"I know that you don't really want my orb. There is

nothing about me you care about."

"I-I—"

"You don't know where Zendora is! Nor do you know Morphaal! If you did, Morphaal would want my orb. And even if you did, you wouldn't give it to him, would you? What if Erich's mind is in that orb?"

Vecto walked closer, hoping that was enough to keep his orb safe from being destroyed.

Tyran looked at the orb and then back at Vecto. "Do you know what you've done to me? Who else can share my pain? Who else will care about me?"

"Tyran, please. Return the orb. Perhaps I can bring Erich back, after all."

Tyran lowered his head, looking at the orb, and laughed hysterically.

"No, no. An object cannot hold a soul. Your orb is nothing but machine!" He crushed the orb between both hands and formed energy around it.

"No!" Vecto yelled. His plan didn't work. He shot a pulse wire at his orb and yanked it, but it wouldn't budge. Tyran held tight as zero point energy melted its valignium casing.

"I wonder what makes you tick," Tyran said. His body glowed red as he forced his energy to the orb.

"Stop it!" Vecto yelled. With his other armlet, he shot pulse wires at Tyran's body and activated the pulse energy.

Tyran was unfazed by it all. Instead, a smile crossed his face as he had a peek inside the orb.

"Energy? Your orb is energy?" The orb glowed white as the rest of the metal casing melted in Tyran's hands. The energy was intense, burning off pieces of his power suit. Skin from Tyran's face flaked off as he stared at the orb of energy and grunted in pain.

"Such—raw power," Tyran said, laboring to breathe. "Such beauty. Such power is not deserved for you. Nor Morphaal—nor anyone for that matter!"

"Leave it alone!" Vecto yelled and ran at Tyran. He tripped up and almost got tangled in his wires. Tyran gasped for air. The armor on his arms peeled off, and his arms burned. His face as well. But he loved the pain.

"To think," Tyran said, "you are not a machine. You only possess machines! Let this be our little secret." Tyran raised the orb in the air.

"What are you doing?" Vecto said. "Erich could be in there!"

Tyran cringed and recoiled, grabbing his head with one hand. "No! Not again!"

White energy swirled from the orb over his body, creating sparks and lighting Tyran on fire. Vecto stumbled up and grabbed the energy orb, trying to pull it from Tyran.

"Let it go or it'll kill you!" Vecto yelled.

The energy encompassed Vecto as well.

Tyran laughed hysterically as his hair burned in flames. "The power, the power!"

Vecto screamed in pain as the energy grew around them and blasted from their bodies.

"We have to contain it!" Vecto yelled.

"No, no. We must destroy it!" Tyran yelled.

"I need it!"

"No one needs it!"

Tyran yanked the orb away and tossed it off the catwalk. He then fired an explosive shell, impacting the orb. It exploded, bursting energy throughout the room. Towering tubes of energy shattered and other explosions followed.

Vecto fell to his knees as energy rained on them,

burning their skin. "What have you done?" he yelled. He formed a mask over his head to protect him.

Tyran curled up in flames, laughing.

Alarms blared and Sarah's choppy voice spoke as if broadcast from a week transmission. "Vecto! Get—of here!"

"No! My orb!"

"Vecto, are—listening to me?!"

"How am I going to return to my body without my orb?"

"Get out of—Vecto!"

"And what about you?"

"Don't worry—me! This ship is—to explode and—can't save me!"

Vecto disconnected the wires he had dangling from his arms and rushed to the console to look at the data.

"Face it, Vecto—not a robot," Sarah said. "—can't download me. Now—"

Tyran laughed and rolled on the floor to put out the flames. More massive tubes exploded as parts of them leaned and crashed on the catwalk.

Vecto stumbled as the catwalk shook.

"We will die together, Erich," Tyran said, his face mutilated. "Me and you, forever in bliss."

Vecto reached down and grabbed Tyran by the collar of his suit. He banged his head against the catwalk.

Tyran smirked. "Your eyes. It's happening."

Vecto slammed him against the catwalk again. He noticed the veins in his arms turning dark—the muscles in his body tensing. Vecto could feel his blood boil and flow through his body like snakes slithering through his veins.

"What's happening to me?" Vecto yelled and slammed Tyran's head.

"It has accepted you," Tyran said and laughed, swirling his head around in dizziness. "You have become me."

Vecto let go of Tyran and looked at his arms and body. He was glowing red. Anger filled his body, smothered with sadness. His mind slipped away, and he snapped. Everything around him blackened. He smelled fire and gases. He felt energy explode around him like a sun going supernova. He knew nothing but what he felt. And he felt the whole ship explode.

Crysilis stood at a viewport from the bridge of his ship, AESS Gyro, watching rubble of the Corona drift in space. Standing beside him was Feit, wearing a white robe Crysilis provided him, and Azmeck, wearing beach shorts and an A-shirt barely covering his wrinkled skin.

"Are there any other survivors?" Feit asked, his arms folded inside his robe's sleeves.

"No," Crysilis said, still looking out the viewport. "Poor Vecto."

"My, my. But if it wasn't for you receiving our distress call, we'd all be dead," Azmeck said, stroking his white beard.

"But I wasn't here to stop Vecto this time," Crysilis said and lowered his head.

"Do you think he has awakened yet?" Azmeck asked.

"Probably," Crysilis said. "And likely in trauma."

"Indeed," Azmeck said. "Perhaps we should avoid telling him what he did."

"If he doesn't remember, he'll eventually find out," Feit said.

"Only time will tell," Crysilis said. He stepped away from the viewport and rested his hands behind his back. "Let's pay him a visit, OK?"

* * *

Vecto awoke to excruciating pain. He looked around him to see that he was in a medical room tied to various machinery. His clothing save for an undergarment was missing, and he could hear the chatter of nurses attending to other patients.

"Are you awake, Erich?" a male nurse asked and approached him.

"Where am I?"

"You've been out for a week," the nurse said as he reviewed his vitals. "We found your body floating in space. If it wasn't for your suit, you'd be dead."

"What happened?"

"Why, the ship exploded."

Vecto sat up and looked at his hands. They were human. All of what happened was real. He was human.

The door opened and in came Dr. Azmeck.

"Ah, Vecto, how do you feel?"

Vecto looked at him with a puzzled look. "What happened to the ship? Where are the others?"

Feit walked in, followed by Crysilis.

"Trip? Cutlass?" Vecto said.

Feit shook his head.

"Chais? Accura?"

Feit lowered his head. "We're the only ones alive. Everyone you see in this room."

Vecto looked around him to see a couple Terran guards and a dozen civilians—men, women, and one boy with a toy visor. Vecto recognized the boy and stood up.

"Be careful," the nurse said. "You're still connected and recovering."

Vecto tore the wires off him.

"Vecto, are you all right?" Crysilis asked.

Vecto walked to the boy and kneeled beside him.

"Can you see me now?" Vecto asked.

The boy looked through his visor and nodded, a tear rolling down his cheek. "Yes, mister. But I can't see Mommy and Daddy."

Vecto paused, not knowing what to say. He stood up, confused on how to respond.

"Did I destroy the ship?" Vecto asked, his back turned to the others.

Crysilis walked up to him and laid a hand on his shoulder. "It wasn't your fault," he said.

"I remember Tyran destroying my orb," Vecto said. "I remember the anger boiling. I did something and blacked out. What have I done?"

Crysilis removed his hand and lowered his head. "Yes, Vecto. You destroyed the ship."

"I killed Trip and Cutlass, Chais and Accura, and Sarah!" Vecto said, turning around. "I even killed Erich and took his body. Why am I alive and not them? Why do I deserve to live?"

"You didn't kill Cutlass," Feit said. "He sacrificed his life to save Trip."

"Only for me to kill him afterward!" Vecto said.

"Calm down, Vecto," Azmeck said. "It was out of your control!"

Vecto grabbed Crysilis by the shoulder. "You're right. I'm out of control." His eyes watered. "Kill me! I don't deserve to live!"

"And what if Erich is trapped inside you?" Azmeck said. "You'd kill him as well!"

Vecto leaned over a bed and grabbed the sheets, clutching them tightly.

"Then put me in jail! I don't know—just stop me from

killing others!"

"And what about Morphaal?" Crysilis said. "Shouldn't we find Zendora and stop *him* from killing others?"

Vecto looked up at him with a tear rolling down his cheek. "Do you really think I can stop him? Look at me!" He raised his arm. "I'm flesh and bone. Morphaal is far more superior!"

"Phantom was flesh, too," Crysilis reminded him.

"And he died."

Crysilis looked away.

Vecto laughed. "Ironic. He died trying to find Zendora."

"Phantom wouldn't have it any other way!" Crysilis said.

"Everyone died because of me!" Vecto slung his arms and smashed it into machinery, then flipped the bed over.

"We need to sedate him!" Dr. Azmeck said.

Vecto spun around and punched Crysilis in his blocky helmet. His fist struck his blue visor but did no damage.

Crysilis stood there, cocked his head, and kicked Vecto.

Vecto bulged over, holding his groin, and threw up.

Crysilis walked away. "All right, he's sedated. Cuff him. We'll take him to Acaterra."

Feit cringed at the sight and looked at Crysilis as he stopped at the door. "Sir, I'd hate to be on your bad side."

"My, my," Azmeck said. "I'm sorry, Vecto."

A Terran guard cuffed Vecto. Vecto looked up, unable to wipe his mouth.

Crysilis looked back to meet his gaze. "As far as the government is concerned, Vecto is dead. Your name is now Erich."

An hour later, Vecto stared out the window of his cell. He watched debris float as the ship jolted and began drifting away from the rubble.

His mind was filled with thoughts, memories of his friends. They were indeed his friends, Vecto thought, no matter how little he knew of them. They were people he cared about.

He remembered his first encounter with Chais. Sure, he was a thief, but he was cunning, quick, and fearless.

Then there was Accura. She sought to kill him because it was her job. She's even had chances to kill him but didn't take them. Although she wouldn't admit it, her time spent following him was to learn about him, not to kill him.

And Trip, he was a genius stuck with a stutter. If only he had lived, he could put his healing powers to more use. Vecto was grateful that he used them to heal Erich. He was grateful that Cutlass looked after him. Although annoying with his pirate speak, he had a heart of gold.

And Tyran ... was there truly a way to save him like Erich believed? Will Vecto become as demented as him and continue to kill others? His friends were dead, and Vecto blamed himself. Leroy was right about his orb. He had life within it. But that life of his destroyed the ship, killing his friends.

He caused this destruction, Vecto thought. He killed hundreds of innocent lives, just like he did to the SS6 trainees. He recalled one of Erich's last words to him. "Promise me you won't kill anyone." It was a promise he couldn't make. Or was it a promise he chose not to make?

Erich's words weighed heavy on him. *If Erich is truly trapped inside me*, Vecto thought, *what would he want him to do?* How would he want Vecto to carry on with his life? Vecto already knew the answer. He watched Erich spare lives, watched him go willing to jail for a crime he didn't commit, watched him forgive others and try to save those who tried to kill him. Vecto knew what he had to do.

"I promise, Erich. I promise."

REID KEMPER

Reid Kemper loves science fiction, anime, superhero movies, and RPG video games. He started writing stories when he created the character Vecto in 1996 at age 12 for a group called the Alpha Squad that he and his friends created. As the collaborative universe grew, so did his love for writing.

You can find him at:
ReidKemper.com
VicsLab.com/members/ReidKemper
Twitter.com/ReidKemper
Facebook.com/ReidKemper
Wattpad.com/ReidKemper

VicsLab.com
Publisher and community for fans of light novels and superhero stories.

Made in the USA
Lexington, KY
26 April 2017